Colours of the Soul

S.E. SMITH

MONTANA
PUBLISHING

Acknowledgments

I would like to thank my husband, Steve, for believing in me and being proud enough of me to give me the courage to follow my dream. I would also like to give a special thank you to my sister and best friend, Linda, who not only encouraged me to write, but who also read the manuscript. Also, to my other friends who believe in me: Julie, Jackie, Christel, Sally, Jolanda, Lisa, Laurelle, Debbie, and Narelle. The girls that keep me going!

And a special thanks to Paul Heitsch, David Brenin, Samantha Cook, Suzanne Elise Freeman, PJ Ochlan, Vincent Fallow, L. Sophie Helbig, and Hope Newhouse, Allison River, and Bethanne Reid—the outstanding voices behind my audiobooks!

– S. E. Smith

Contemporary Romance
COLOURS OF THE SOUL
GIRLS FROM THE STREET BOOK 2
Copyright © 2022 by S.E. Smith
First E-Book Published September 2022
Cover Design by Melody Simmons

Summary: When a mysterious, masked woman in the desert saves his life, a royal sheikh will use all of his resources to find her.

ISBN: 9781956052626 (Amazon Paperback)
ISBN: 9781956052619 (eBook)
ISBN: 9781956052916 (BN Paperback)

Romance (love, explicit sexual content) | Contemporary | Action/Adventure

Published by Montana Publishing, LLC
& SE Smith of Florida Inc. www.sesmithfl.com

Contents

Synopsis

She was born on the streets; he was born to rule...

Idella goes by one name only in the glamorous world of music. Her sultry voice mesmerizes millions, her albums have gone platinum, and her elusiveness is legendary. However, the version of herself that truly drives her goes by another name—Dallas. She's an assassin employed to eliminate some of the worst criminals in the world.

Sheikh Tarek Saif-Ad-Din understands that power and money can corrupt. It is his job to ensure the safety of his people, his country, and his royal family. After an attack leaves him near death, he swears he hears the voice of an *'amirat khurafiat alsahra'*—a desert fairy princess.

Helping a wounded prince was not part of the plan. Her targets were the insurrectionists. She was supposed to prevent them from gaining control of the largest production of microchips in the world at any cost. Even if both the first and second born sons die, another in the royal family line would become heir and the country would stabilize. Yet—she can't leave Tarek to die.

In a dangerous dance between two identities, Idella must decide if she can trust Tarek enough to reveal who she really is—a singer, an assassin, and the woman who loves him. If she can't, this mission may be final in more ways than one.

A NY Times and USA Today bestselling author, the internationally acclaimed S.E. Smith presents a new story with her signature humor and unpredictable twists! Exciting adventure, hot romance, and iconic characters have won her a legion of fans. Over TWO MILLION books sold!

One

Aljibal Alsawda'

(Black Mountains of Jawahir)

"We have to go. There is no time to save him," Raja impatiently said, pulling on her arm as he warily scanned the area around them.

"I have to stop the bleeding. He'll die if I don't," Dallas calmly retorted, laying her sniper rifle beside her on the dry, hard-packed sand and rock-strewn ground.

"Then he dies. The Royal Guards are dead. We will lose our targets in the mountains if we don't leave now!"

Dallas glanced up at the steep hill. Regret coursed through her. She had sent a message warning of the attack, but it arrived too late, and they had been too far away to reach the convoy before it started. The volley of gunfire had faded several minutes ago, leaving behind a desert painted in blood and filled with death.

She looked down at the barely conscious man. Determination filled her as she slid her sharp knife from the sheath at her waist. She knew who he was—Sheikh Tarek, the second son of King Melik and Queen Ihab Saif-Ad-Din of Jawahir. Their handlers would consider Tarek's death collateral damage. Even the capture of the Royal Heir, Sheikh Qadir, was not their concern. Raja and Dallas were here to eliminate Colin and Anderson Coldhouse.

Their objective was clear—and they were explicitly ordered to not deviate from it. Dallas knew she should leave Tarek to his fate, but she couldn't. She had met him before—in her life as Idella.

She turned to Raja with an impatient scowl. Orders be damned, she would do what she could to save Tarek.

"Get me the medical kit," she ordered in a tone that said she would tolerate no more arguments.

"You are going to get us killed," Raja grumbled even as he twisted and rose to his feet.

A rueful smile curved her lips when Raja darted up the steep incline to retrieve the pack she had dropped during the conflict. Despite Raja's fierce expression, she knew that he, too, would be bothered by leaving an injured man behind.

Especially when the man is one of the good guys.

Tarek was pale. Dallas bent over his inert body and cut a thin line in his shirt and pants where the blood had soaked through. She peeled back the fabric to reveal his wounds.

Grabbing a clean bandana from a pouch at her waist, she sliced it in half and folded the pieces into squares before applying them to the two bullet wounds. She kept the pressure firm and constant as she calmly reassured Tarek that he would be alright, though she was pretty sure he was too out of it to hear her.

Both wounds were serious. She wasn't sure which one was worse, the one to his lower left abdomen or the one to his leg. Either could be fatal if a major artery or organ had been hit. Fortunately, the blood seeping from his abdomen was bright red, not a deep ruby color. This gave her hope that no major organs were damaged.

"Qadir…" Tarek weakly mumbled. "W-what…?"

"He's alive," she said as she gently brushed sand from his cheek.

"Who… are you?"

She didn't answer. Instead, she impatiently looked up, searching for Raja. She breathed a sigh of relief when she saw him sliding back down the slope toward them. He dropped the pack next to her, opened it, and pulled out their medical field kit.

"Set up the saline line."

Raja looked at her mutinously for a moment before he did as instructed, cursing under his breath all the while. Most equipment could be traced, but she made sure that everything she used couldn't be. Her sudden act of compassion would not reveal their identities to the royal family of Jawahir.

Raja connected the tubing to the saline bag, expertly cleaned a section on Tarek's arm with alcohol, and inserted the needle into his vein. Dallas ripped Tarek's black shirt wider to give them room to work.

"How bad?" Raja asked.

"Bullet is still in him. It doesn't look like it hit any major organs."

"Let me look. You're right. You take care of this while I take care of his leg."

She nodded. While she was good with some advanced first aid, Raja could do field surgery if pushed. He had patched her up more than once.

"We're going to catch hell if they get away. It took us a week to track them this far. How long do you think it'll take to find them again?" Raja grumbled as he worked.

"Shut up."

Raja glared at her but kept silent as he injected a mild sedative into the port.

Tarek grabbed her wrist. Even half dead, his grip was strong.

"D-don't."

"Too late. You'll thank us later." She smiled before she remembered that he wouldn't be able to see it behind her face covering. Only her eyes were visible. She had removed her sunglasses so she could examine his wounds with no distortion.

"Who...." his voice slurred before his head rolled to the side.

"I hear helicopters approaching," Raja growled.

She finished applying the bandage to Tarek's leg. "Done. Let's get this cleaned up and get out of here."

What they had done for Tarek would give the medics a better chance of keeping him alive until they reached the hospital. It eased her mind.

"You're going soft on me," Raja said as they stored their equipment in the camouflaged backpack and picked up their weapons.

"How many men did I just kill?" she quietly asked.

"The mission—"

"There's no way to know if Colin Coldhouse was with the first group we encountered," she reasoned.

"...Ok, yes, I did not see Colin and there was never a clear shot to Anderson. It *is* hard to kill someone you can't see," he grudgingly admitted.

Her lips twitched at his concession. "Tarek's guards?"

"I confirmed. No survivors," he quietly replied.

She nodded, pushing away the feelings of regret, and moved out. They circled the slope, keeping low and near the cover of rocks and limited vegetation until they crossed the road and hopped into their electric all-terrain vehicles. They followed the less discernable paths, and ten minutes later, they found shelter in a narrow cave high above where the attack had occurred.

Dallas peered through her scope, watching the first wave of Royal Military arrive. "It looks like we should hang tight for a while longer than I hoped," Raja said.

"Yes. Coldhouse will have to do the same—at least until dark."

The medic team scurried over the side of the hill. Several minutes later they emerged with Tarek on a stretcher, placed him into the waiting helicopter, and took off. She followed the helicopter until it disappeared from sight. She flexed her stiff shoulders, breathing in deep breaths as her tension eased a little.

She closed the cover on the scope and removed her camouflage netting before scooting back and seeking shelter in the shade of the cave. Almost immediately, the temperature dropped fifteen degrees.

"Here." Raja held out a bottle of water.

She accepted it and relaxed against the uneven wall. Pulling her face covering down, she drank deeply from the bottle. When she was done, she set it down next to her and leaned her head back. She closed her eyes, unaware of the slight smile on her lips as she replayed in her mind the first time that she met Tarek.

Three years ago

Colours Nightclub, New York City

Idella felt a heightened, tingling sensation that wasn't her normal awareness of being watched. She was an international star and she was singing on stage with an amazing group of musicians; of course every eye in the club she owned was on her. Still, this kind of awareness was… different.

Her body swayed with the music as she sang, and her performance commanded the room's attention. It was more than just her voice. Her body was a masterpiece as well. With silver heels adding several inches to her height, she was six feet tall. Her sequined silver gown hugged her slender figure, leaving one shoulder bare. The shimmering gown contrasted beautifully against her mocha-crème skin. The side slit stopped at the top of her thigh, showing a generous length of her long leg. There were hard-won muscles within her slender form, which meant her curves were very well defined.

Tall, lithe, and dressed as she was tonight, she was a jaw-droppingly gorgeous woman. Her audience had been captivated from the moment she stepped on-stage—but in just the last couple of minutes, something had changed. The sensation was almost as if she was being hunted. Every nerve was alight with the anticipation of a life-or-death encounter.

A specific motion of her hand put Raja on alert. Within minutes, he would know the history of every person in the building. She shifted ever so slightly on the stage, scanning the room.

Her singing was still laden with the appropriate emotion and skill, her years of training serving her well as her focus lingered on each table long enough to make the people sitting at them pause and take notice. She assessed each person as friend or foe before moving onto the next one.

One of the hostesses was leading a group up the staircase to the dining level. Idella's lips curved when she saw the tiny woman in tattered jeans. Aimee Wheels was an enigma and a welcome friend to the club. Idella turned her attention to Aimee's companions.

A flash of shock registered when she recognized the first and second born sons of the Jawahir royal family. Idella had never met any of them personally, but of course she knew of their power and wealth, and she knew there had been an attempted assassination of Sheikh Qadir just a week ago at the Harris building downtown. Aimee had saved Sheikh Qadir's life.

She carefully noted the body language of the group. It appeared Aimee was in a romantic relationship with Sheikh Qadir, the first-born of the

Saif-Ad-Din family. Accompanying them was Sheikh Tarek. The heated awareness running through her body intensified as she studied his handsome face and lean, yet muscular body. A shaft of feminine appreciation swept through her. The emotion startled her as she was usually immune to such physical responses.

She knew Tarek was a Cabinet member and Head of Jawahir Military Intelligence. He had graduated from Oxford and held advanced degrees from Princeton. He had also served in the Jawahir Special Forces.

She forced her eyes away from him and finished the last line of the song. As applause broke out, she stepped back from the microphone, bowed, waved to the band, and gracefully departed the stage.

She was curious about why they were here—and what kind of problems the royal brothers would bring to her sanctuary. Raja met up with her the moment she stepped behind the curtain, his brow furrowed with displeasure.

"They are with Aimee," she soothed.

"You know who we suspect is behind the attack on Sheikh Qadir," he murmured.

She palmed the keypad to her private spiral staircase and pushed the door open. "Then perhaps tonight is a good time to get more information," she said.

Raja followed and they began climbing, the door soundlessly swinging shut behind them. When he touched her arm, however, she turned to face him. They were eye-to-eye with him standing on the step below her.

The tabloids claimed Raja and Idella were lovers. Nothing could be further from the truth. He was her bodyguard, her friend, and her partner in the shadow life she led. He was the Hamlet to her Dallas.

Their relationship had formed in the most unlikely of ways. They were born in very different places, but Harlem Jones had collected children from around the world, including Raja and Idella. Those that didn't break from his training eventually went on to do great things. They became senators, preachers, influential artists—wherever their gifts could take them, Harlem would make sure they got there. Their 'Father' could make any position and contact beneficial to himself.

Raja preferred to pretend that he wasn't a leader, but Idella knew he wouldn't be able to run from his past forever. In some ways, his early childhood was far more tragic than her own. He'd had more to lose.

"Be careful, Idella," he quietly warned.

She gave him a small smile. "Always."

They parted, Idella emerging on the second level and Raja returning to the first. Idella moved the decorative curtain that camouflaged the door back to its proper place and stepped out of the shallow alcove, requesting a glass of white Zinfandel from a passing server. She warmly greeted diners who were in awe at meeting *the* Idella.

"Thank you, Karly," she murmured when the server brought her the glass of wine.

Tarek sat alone. A swift perusal showed Aimee and Qadir heading for the dance floor and the royal bodyguards splitting up to cover both brothers. Idella returned her gaze to Tarek, and her eyes locked with his.

Heat rose in her cheeks and Idella swore a riot of butterflies invaded her stomach. The intensity of the desire in his eyes made her almost look down to see if she was still wearing her evening gown. Instead, she maintained eye contact with him, walked over to his table, and gracefully slid into one of the empty seats with a practiced smile.

"Welcome to my club, Sheikh Saif-Ad-Din," she greeted.

His eyes flickered with surprise. "Idella," he murmured. "Please, call me Tarek."

Her name on his lips sent a shaft of unexpected need through her. Raja's cautioning words flashed through her mind.

Over the years, she had met her share of the handsomest men alive, and they had desired her. Offers of money, diamonds, anything she wanted could have been hers for the taking—if she had been for sale. She wasn't and never would be.

"Aimee is a beautiful woman," she commented, sipping her wine and studying his face.

"She is very unusual," Tarek agreed.

"I believe she saved your brother last week. Do you know who was behind the attempt?" she asked.

"No, why do you ask?" he inquired.

She almost smiled. It was exactly how she would have answered if she were in his place. She shrugged.

"After dealing with many attempts on my own life," she briefly paused when she noticed the way anger flared in his dark brown eyes and his relaxed posture stiffened slightly at her comment before she smoothly continued, "I'm well aware of how dangerous being a person of interest can be. I like to know who my threats are. I'm sure you and your brother feel the same."

"You've received threats?" he asked quietly.

She shrugged again and looked away. "More than just threats, I'm afraid," she casually replied.

"I'm glad you survived." She looked into his eyes, and for a moment, she felt as if she was trapped in a cage with a hungry lion. She shook the image away and smiled.

"What brings you to New York?"

Their conversation varied after that. No matter what they talked about, though, raw sexual hunger laced their interaction like a secret dance. Idella held out as long as she could before she escaped.

Her heart pounded and her whole body buzzed with awareness as she sashayed away from him with a deceptive calm. A gazelle knew when to run from a predator. Still, she couldn't help but imagine what it would be like to be captured by a man who fired such a deep yearning inside her.

Or how dangerous the outcome!

Two

Present day:

"Dallas, we're clear to move out," Raja murmured.

Idella woke immediately and rose to her feet. She retrieved the night vision goggles from her bag. Raja checked the ATVs and secured the gear while she completed a perimeter check. They worked together silently, each knowing the other would efficiently complete their own tasks.

Ten minutes later, they were following the barely discernible path, searching for Anderson and Colin Coldhouse. Idella knew they couldn't afford for her to be distracted, yet, as hard as she tried to deny it, she knew the first thing she would do when she had a chance was check on Tarek.

Voices mixed with the flashing lights, creating an overwhelming and confusing combination. Tarek fought against whatever drug had been pumped into his veins, trying to process what was going on. Flashes of memories swam to the surface of his brain: helicopter rotors, men's voices, military uniforms. Someone was speaking to him, a woman's voice, but the words weren't registering. There was pressure on his side and leg, but no pain.

He faded in and out of consciousness until awareness suddenly struck him as he was lifted out of the helicopter. He tried to sit up, but a firm hand prevented him.

"Qadir," Tarek said.

"They are searching for him. There's nothing you can do now. Do you know who helped you?"

That deep voice belonged to Junayd, Tarek's twenty-eight-year-old brother. He was a doctor.

Tarek licked his dry lips. "An... *'amirat khurafiat alsahra'*," he croaked out before the darkness took him again.

Time passed slowly. He heard his brother making demands. He smelled the antiseptic of the hospital. Blinding light forced him to keep his eyes closed. His body alternated between being too cold or too hot.

Threaded through each wave were memories of a woman's soothing voice telling him that everything would be alright. That help was on the way.

Though the voice was muffled, something inside him connected with it. He knew that voice. Except that was impossible. There was no way it could have been. But those eyes... her beautiful, exotic eyes—

"Idella!" he gasped, struggling to sit up.

"Take it easy, Tarek," Junayd said soothingly.

He blinked, trying to focus, and relaxed back on the bed when he recognized it was Junayd blocking his view of the room. He turned his head, looking at the monitoring equipment attached to him.

"How bad?" he asked, his throat dry and sore.

Junayd chuckled with relief. "You'll live. The bullet in your side wasn't as bad as it could have been. The one in your leg nicked an artery. You'll have to take it easy for a while, but you'll be as good as new eventually."

Tarek's mind was beginning to clear.

"And Qadir? Does he live?" he quietly demanded.

"Yes. He's even in a little better condition than you."

Relief swept through his body, leaving him weak. He closed his eyes, fighting against fatigue. His brother's firm fingers on his wrist caused him to startle.

"What are you doing?" he demanded, his voice threadier than expected.

"I don't know, acting like a doctor," Junayd retorted with a smile.

"Mother must have dropped you on your head when you were a kid," he muttered.

Junayd released his wrist and raised an eyebrow. "No, that was you and Qadir. Speaking of Mother, I need to notify the family. They have been terrified. I kept reassuring them you were too stubborn to die. Father only convinced Mother to return home about an hour ago. She has been by your side for the last three days."

Tarek gripped his brother's wrist to keep him from leaving. Junayd turned back to him. He fought to form the words in his head.

"What is it?" Junayd asked with concern.

"My wounds…. Who….?"

"Well, that's the mystery, isn't it? Someone patched you up in the field, but all the guards were dead and Qadir was missing." He shook his head. "Whoever attended you had the medical training and field experience to keep you from bleeding out. They slowed the bleeding, raised your leg above your heart, and hooked you to an IV. Blood tests revealed a small amount of morphine in your system."

"There were two people. I couldn't tell what they looked like, they kept their faces covered. One of them was a woman," he said.

"That must be your *'amirat khurafiat alsahra'*," Junayd said with a gentle smile.

"What did you say?"

Junayd grinned. "Your desert fairy princess. You said your *'amirat khurafiat alsahra'* helped you."

Tarek closed his eyes, desperately trying to bring that moment into focus. His brain refused to cooperate and he silently cursed. Three days! He had lost three days of his life. Opening his eyes, he stared up at his brother's concerned face.

"Keep the materials they used on me. I want to see if I can trace them," he tiredly ordered.

"I will," Junayd promised.

The door opened and Tarek wanted to groan when he saw his mother and father's exhausted faces.

"Oh, Tarek!" Ihab exclaimed, her eyes filling with joyful tears at the sight of him awake.

Dr. Fuah gave Tarek an apologetic look as his parents came to his side and his mother held his hand.

"Your mother refused to rest," King Melik Saif-Ad-Din gruffly stated, his voice filled with barely-concealed emotion.

Junayd cleared his throat. "As his doctor, I think a short visit will help you all, but only ten minutes. Tarek needs to rest, and so do you. I'd like to talk to Dr. Fuah about his patient."

"Qadir?" his mother worriedly inquired.

"It is nothing to worry about. We are debating if we should sedate him to keep him from charging off and doing something stupid like getting himself killed," Junayd replied, wincing when he saw his mother's expression. "That was probably not the best thing to say."

"Qadir will recover, your Highness," Dr. Fuah gently reassured her.

Ihab sent a grateful smile at Dr. Fuah and scowled at Junayd. Tarek chuckled, then winced and reached for his side.

"I want a full report on everything, Junayd," he called after his younger brother.

"It can wait until tomorrow," Junayd replied.

Tarek laid his head back against the pillows. He wanted peace and quiet, but he knew his mother and father needed reassurance that he would be fine. He watched his brother and Dr. Fuah as they walked past the window of the private room in the palace's medical suite.

He had lost three days. Three days in which the woman and her companion could be anywhere—and three days in which those responsible for the attack could have gotten away.

Idella tiredly looked up from her laptop when Raja entered the room. The drab hotel room contained two single beds, a spartan bathroom, and a window that overlooked the bustling street below. They had arrived in Yasir, the Simdan city closest to Jawahir, a few hours earlier after traveling through the night.

"What did you find out?" she asked.

There were lines of strain around Raja's mouth. She knew he would rather be in the burning fires of hell than here. Her heart ached for him, but she kept her sympathy from showing. He would never accept it.

"Two helicopters picked up a group of foreigners outside the city late last night." He dropped a bag on the scarred table. "Dinner."

She watched him walk into the bathroom and shut the door. A peek in the bag revealed bread, fruit, cheese, and several bottles of water. The poverty in Simdan reminded her of her own life—before Harlem.

It wasn't something she thought about often. She had stopped hiding away food a long time ago, finally secure in the fact that she wouldn't go hungry anymore. No, with Harlem, she'd had to fight to survive in other ways. They both had.

She didn't cling to any reminders of her past. Her club, Colours, was named to be the opposite of the business of death. It was vibrancy in the spotlight. It was the full spectrum of emotion. It was a world that was distinct from her life as an American assassin.

Even her code name was randomly chosen by the throw of a knife. It was not a place or a person that was special to her. Raja's chosen name, however, was a different story—not that he'd told her many details when they were growing up.

They had been in Harlem's care since she was nine and Raja was twelve. Harlem died when she was sixteen and Raja nineteen, and by then, they had become an incredible team—too valuable an asset for the CIA to ignore. Now, at twenty-six, she had seen her share of the horrors that humans could inflict on one another. What Harlem hadn't killed, the government was trying to—in the both of them.

She dragged her unfocused stare away from the closed bathroom door and keyed into a separate VPN address. Her fingers flew across the keyboard. A symbol of a bug crawling across the screen appeared. In seconds, millions of little bugs began appearing. Idella grinned when the bugs merged into a huge happy face.

Hi, Dallas. What's up?

Hey, Bugs. I need help.

What's the mission?

Need info on three. Colin Coldhouse, Anderson Coldhouse, and Andrius Bronislav. Location and movement.

Cost you a coin.

One now, one on confirmation of info.

Twenty minutes for initial

Nevermind, Bronislav is in Moscow at the following location. Guy really should get better security.

Idella chuckled. Images from a government satellite appeared. She printed out several of Bronislav entering his heavily secured mansion.

Picked up a communication thread. Sending audio. Anderson is in some place called Simdan. I'll have to check it out. Colin is buzzing to Moscow. Emotion analyzer detects stress. He must be in deep shit.

Can you narrow down Anderson's location?

Target moving. Sending last known location.

Payment sent.

Thought you were going to verify first.

Trust you.

The bugs formed one huge smile before creating hundreds of little smiley faces on the screen. Seconds later, nothing but the cursor flashed as the last bug waved goodbye.

Idella shook her head. Bugs was an enigma. She had no idea who the hacker was, only that Bugs had information, or could get information, on anyone on the planet. Idella could count on one hand the number of people that she genuinely trusted in this world. Bugs, Raja, Aimee, and Midnight were pretty much it.

Midnight was another of Harlem's recruits. She had vanished the night Harlem was murdered. Idella didn't know if she was the one who killed him, she only knew that Midnight had saved her life and was given a scar for her trouble.

Idella closed the laptop and looked up when Raja entered the room again, this time wearing a pair of fatigue pants and nothing else. He was rubbing his damp hair with a towel.

Her affectionate smile faded when she saw a fresh wound on his back as he moved past her.

"What happened?" she asked.

He stiffened and turned so she couldn't see the cut that spanned from his shoulder to his hip. "Nothing."

She narrowed her eyes. It wasn't deep, but it still needed to be cared for. She rose from her seat and withdrew the medical kit from her backpack.

"Turn around," she ordered.

She sat on the edge of the bed and opened the kit. He looked like he was about to argue before he turned his back to her and sat where she could easily tend to him.

"I had a disagreement with a couple of thieves," he said.

"Do we need to move out?"

"They ran off. I didn't kill them," he grudgingly replied.

She cleaned the wound with disinfectant even though he had just showered, applied a thin coating of antibiotic cream and a thick pad over the deepest cut, and then wrapped his chest with gauze. In this climate, the wound needed to be protected.

"I don't need all of this," he grumbled as she wound the gauze.

"Think of it as extra padding so the next time you get in a knife fight you'll have more protection," she replied.

He grunted. She smiled at his grouchy response.

"Colin has traveled to meet with Bronislav in Moscow. Anderson is still here. I have his last location."

"I'll go check it out," Raja said.

"I think this time I should be the one to take a look," she replied with a pointed glare at the medical supplies she had just used.

Raja paused, then sighed with resignation. "*We* will go check it out."

Three

Frustration coursed through Tarek and he rose to his feet so quickly that his chair fell backwards. His nurse hurried to the balcony to check on him. He waved the man away with an impatient hand.

"I've got this," he growled.

The nurse looked from him to the chair with an uncertain expression before he bowed and solemnly backed away. Tarek sighed as his irritation melted to remorse. The nurse was just doing what he had been ordered to do. It wasn't the man's fault that Tarek didn't want him there.

He righted the chair before he moved to the banister, gripped the concrete railing, and stared blindly down at the gardens below. His memories of the attack two weeks ago were still unclear—except for one voice. *Her* voice. It played in his mind over and over and over.

A movement in the garden caught his attention. Qadir, Aimee, and his mother were walking together. He breathed deeply, calming his mind and body as he had done thousands of times before a mission. He needed to remember every detail.

"Everything will be alright. Help is on the way."

Her voice cut through the intense pain. He remembered clinging to the husky sound like a drowning man to a lifeline. Her face had been shielded but not her eyes. She had removed her sunglasses and he remembered her eyes—hazel, almond-shaped eyes framed by long lush dark lashes that he swore he knew.

He slammed his fist against the railing. "Impossible," he growled.

Idella could not have been the woman. Idella was an internationally acclaimed singer. She owned a nightclub in Harlem, dressed in sexy, shimmering gowns and wore delicate, designer heels. He must have been hallucinating. It was the only rational possibility. His thoughts turned to her companion, but he didn't remember much about the man.

While Tarek was recovering in the medical suite, one of his Intelligence agents, Selima, had unexpectedly met with his mysterious rescuers. The man and woman who saved him had also helped rescue Qadir. The woman's alias was Dallas, the man was Hamlet. The physical description of the two was bare bones. They both had kept their faces covered—including their eyes—and wore gloves and military fatigues. The woman was American. Selima wasn't sure about the man.

After Qadir was safe, the scene was analyzed. There were a lot of dead, mostly Anderson's people. Six of Qadir's kidnappers were shot with a SSG 69 sniper rifle with .308 Winchester rounds. The same was found at the scene where Tarek was wounded and Qadir kidnapped. The bullets had disintegrated on impact, making them untraceable. There were no bullet casings.

Others at the scene of Qadir's rescue had reported seeing Dallas and Hamlet slice into the throats of Coldhouse's people. Those two were military or had received military training. They were also gone before the first members of the Royal Military touched the ground, as was Anderson. Subsequent searches for them and Anderson came up empty. It had been almost two weeks of this, and Tarek's people hadn't found them.

He ran his hand through his short black hair. The wound on his side protested the movement, reminding him that he still had work to do in order to recover. He reached for his cane. The nurse, ever-present, appeared in the doorway. He started to scowl at the man before he forced himself to relax.

"I'm ready for physical therapy," he gritted out.

"Yes, sire," the nurse said with a cautious smile.

"Anything?" Raja's voice was quiet in her ear-piece.

"I glimpsed him, but he is staying away from the window."

Dallas felt tension humming through her whole body. Anderson was playing it cautious. He had peered through the curtain of the window, keeping most of his body sheltered by the thick stone and mortar wall. She barely had time to confirm his identity before he disappeared. In the hour that she had been staring through her rifle's sight, he had not looked out again. Raja kept an eye on the other exits.

A movement in the street caught her attention. She realized that it was the local police at the same time her satellite phone vibrated.

> Red alert. Local PD offered huge $$ to
> cover AC.

The little bug running in a circle indicated who the message was from. Dallas smiled. It was good to have someone like Bugs watching her back. She breathed and scanned the area. More officers were arriving.

"Hamlet, local assets are protecting the target. Two heading your way."

"Confirmed. Return to base," he replied.

Dallas waited until Raja was clear before she scooted back, dismantled her rifle, placed it in the case, and headed for the stairs. She was a step above the platform for the next level when she caught sight of two men climbing the staircase. They wore the green uniform of the Simdan police force.

So much for exiting the easy way, she thought.

Sliding the straps of her case onto her shoulders, she turned and retraced her steps to the roof. The two blocks of apartment buildings were connected to each other. She moved to the side opposite of the busy street and looked over the side. The neighboring building's roof was clear of everything but a long clothesline full of freshly washed clothes. It was about a twelve-foot drop to get there.

She sat on the edge, gripped one of the pipes that ran from this roof down to the next, and slid down, jumping the last couple of feet. She landed, hurried across the roof, and entered the rooftop stairwell, adjusting her headscarf as she went.

Minutes later, she joined the foot traffic on the busy street, cautiously walking two blocks of main roads and alleys, using the crowd to her advantage whenever possible. She paused at the top of a flight of stairs to survey the street. The air was thick with the fumes from cars, the oppressive heat, and the haze of sand.

She crossed the road and stepped through the open door of her hotel. The adjacent café meant there were several patrons enjoying their coffee. Young men in traditional throbes chatted with guests. A woman covered from head-to-toe in a flowing robe swept sand from the intricately tiled floor.

Idella followed the usual safety procedures as she climbed to the fourth floor, walked to their room, and used a gadget to make sure there was no one inside before she entered.

Raja hadn't made it back yet.

Once inside the room, she resisted the urge to contact him, instead shrugging off the straps to her rifle case and keeping busy by changing her clothes and refreshing herself. She stared at her reflection in the aged mirror.

In two days, she had to be in London for a concert. For appearance's sake, she couldn't cancel. She pushed away from the sink and returned to the room.

The door opened. Her hand instinctively moved to the pistol tucked in the waistband of her trousers, but she relaxed her pose immediately when she saw who it was.

"I was getting worried," she said.

Raja grunted in response. She silently watched him as he discarded his head-covering, outer robes, and weapons before he fell onto the bed and laid his arm over his eyes.

She didn't push him to explain his mood. No explanation was needed. Simdan was Raja's country. This was the country he was destined to rule—a destiny stolen from him when he was a boy. His uncle had murdered Raja's mother, father, older sister, and younger brother.

If Sheikh Zulfirquar Kaffir ever discovered that Raja had not only survived, but was back in Simdan, he would send the entire Simdan army after him. The return of the true King of Simdan would be devastating to Kaffir—and Raja, if he were caught.

Raja needed his space and Idella willingly gave it to him. She retrieved the laptop and opened it. Biting her lower lip, she peeked out from under her eyelashes to make sure that Raja hadn't moved before typing in a search for Tarek.

A wave of despair struck her when she saw all the beautiful women linked to him. The man was a *slut*! There were many, many women, and none of his relationships lasted more than three months. Also, he had to be filthy rich to pay for all the accessories the women gushed about. Third, he might be handsome and shrewd, but he was not the kind of guy that she would ever bring home to meet Raja—which meant he was off limits.

Maybe this is why Raja suggested I just let Tarek die in the first place, she thought miserably, leaning forward to rest her chin on her palm.

"I can feel your freak-out from over here," Raja dryly commented, not looking at her.

Idella blushed and clicked out of her search. Raja still had his arm across his eyes. She *hated* when he did things like this. She snapped the computer closed.

"I was checking to see how Tarek and Qadir were doing," she lied defensively.

Raja's chest shook with his silent laughter. He dropped his arm to his side and sat up. She looked away, her cheeks still burning.

"I remember when you met him three years ago. I thought I was going to have to call the fire department," he teased.

Idella stood up, suddenly filled with nervous energy. She didn't want to think about her reaction to Tarek or what could have happened between them. Nothing came of it because they had all believed Aimee was murdered. Poor Qadir had grieved so hard that he seemed to be a shell of himself. Tarek brought his brother back to Jawahir, promising to bring the culprits to justice.

Even with Idella's contacts, it had taken almost two years to discover that Aimee was alive and in the protective custody of the U.S. Marshals Service. Bugs had been the one to tell her.

Since Idella was chasing the same well-connected criminals Tarek was targeting, part of her hoped she would run into him—and had kept hoping, even as years passed. She had never felt this way with anyone else. It was just him.

"There was no fire," she dully stated, walking over to peer out of the window.

Raja leaned back against the pillows and gently said, "There was for you."

Tears blurred her vision for a moment before she blinked them away. Harlem said tears should only be used to manipulate or deceive, never for pain, fear, or love. She bowed her head, turning her grief at the emptiness of her life into anger.

"I hate him," she growled. "Harlem. I hate what he turned us into."

Raja raised his eyebrows, then silently slid off the bed, came to the window, and wrapped his arms around her. Seconds passed before she relaxed in his embrace. This life would be unbearable if not for Raja.

"We have good reason to hate him," he said, "but he also saved our lives."

"Death might have been more merciful," she said. "This half-life..." She swallowed and didn't continue that train of thought.

His arms tightened around her. "You are successful. You could tell the agency today that you are retiring and they would have to let you go."

"You could do the same. You could take back your country," she countered. "You have the resources, both financially and politically, to do that."

It was an old argument, and he reacted like he always did. He stiffened and moved away, a mask of indifference settling over his features.

"I'm sorry, Raja," she murmured regretfully. "I shouldn't have said that."

He shoved his hands into the front pockets of his trousers. "I took my time coming back to our room because I had to see... to hear... what the people, my people, were saying. My uncle has ruined this country. He cares nothing for those that are sick, hungry, old. There is no education for the children. A generation is being lost because of his greed." He savagely slashed the air with his hand to emphasize his point.

"Oh," she said softly, the single word conveying her compassion.

"You're right. Harlem did want us to live a half-life. A life with no love, only success as weapons that someone *else* would wield, but he isn't here any longer—and we are too strong now for the chains our puppet-masters hold!"

Pride and love swelled inside Idella. Whatever Raja heard and saw today had severed that last, fragile chain Harlem had wound around him. She belatedly realized that she had broken her last chain as well, the moment she chose Tarek's life over the mission.

"What are you going to do?" she asked.

Raja's dark blue eyes glittered with determination. "We are going to finish our assignment—eliminate the Coldhouse brothers and Bronislav. Then I will return to Simdan and take back what rightfully belongs to my people and what belongs to me."

She touched his arm. "I'll be there for you," she promised.

A slight smile curved his lips. "No hidden dreams of your own?" He held her gaze with eyes that saw too much.

She gave a small smile in return and bowed her head. "I'll finish this mission, more out of revenge than because of any order, and once we're finished, who knows? Maybe I'll see if I can fan the flames with Tarek."

Raja's smile was half grimace. She almost laughed at his struggle to be supportive.

"You might get burned," he warned.

"I think it is Tarek Saif-Ad-Din who should be worried about that," she said defiantly.

Raja pulled her back into his arms and they drew strength from each other as they had done countless times before.

"You know if he breaks your heart, I'll have to kill him, don't you?"

Idella chuckled. "Hopefully that won't be necessary."

Four

Two days later, Tarek was in London. It was against the better judgment of Junayd and Dr. Fuah, but he had to know if he was going crazy. Every piece of intel indicated that Idella had been at her club in New York during his attack. There had been no flight plans filed to Jawahir. No overseas trips until this one.

His chest tightened when the lights dimmed and the music started. A cloud of fog appeared, and Idella emerged from it, rising ten feet above the stage on an elevated platform. She was silhouetted by the red lights behind her, and the overall effect made it look as if she were rising out of flames.

Then... she began to sing. Her sultry voice sent invisible silken threads winding around him. The power behind her words caused goosebumps to rise along his arms. She slowly descended the steps to the stage floor as she sang of unbreaking her heart, filling it with joy and love. As if she knew he was there, her eyes turned to him and she lifted one slender arm as if reaching for him.

He sat forward, his eyes locked on her shimmering form. Her hair was a wild mane of large curls that he wanted to run his fingers through. She wore a white beaded gown that looked as if a million stars had been captured in the soft fabric. The gown was a halter. If he unfastened it, it would fall to her waist, revealing her beautiful bare breasts. They would be the warm, soft color of milk chocolate. A cut-out along the side of her dress made his mind go wild with fantasies.

He was mesmerized by her, and he was done waiting for a convenient time to chase his heart's desire. After almost dying, he wanted to grasp life with both hands and hold on to Idella with everything he possessed.

He looked up with irritation when his bodyguard entered the box in the middle of Idella's last song, but when the man handed him a sealed envelope, the emotion was forgotten.

Tarek and his bodyguards followed a roadie to a service elevator. He leaned on the cane as his leg protested the fact that he had been sitting for too long. The loud thunder of applause alerted him that the show was over.

The elevator doors opened, and as they moved down the corridor, people moved out of the way to allow the group to pass. A wave of intrigued whispers followed in their wake until they arrived at Idella's dressing room.

"She'll be with you shortly," the young man said with a formal bow.

Tarek entered the room. It was surprisingly large. A rack of gowns was situated along the wall closest to the door. There was a vanity table with adjustable lighting, a folding privacy screen, a bathroom with a shower, and a sitting area. The walls were bare of any photos, though he could see the hooks in the walls that would allow them to be displayed.

He heard a sudden commotion outside the room, and he turned as the door opened and Idella stepped inside. She quietly dismissed the three women who were anxiously standing outside the door, and then she closed and locked the door. She leaned back against it and smiled at him.

"I'm glad you came," she said.

He didn't hesitate a moment before stepping forward and capturing her upturned lips.

The moment their lips connected, he was flooded with desire, and she pulled him close with an urgency that mirrored his. His tongue stroked hers, and it was as if he were a dying man who found an oasis in the middle of the desert.

His cane was forgotten, falling against the wall while Tarek leaned against Idella's soft curves, pressing her against the door. They fit together perfectly.

Her hands slid along his side, and paused over his wound. She ended their kiss, her eyes locked on his in a silent question.

"I'm fine," he said. He breathed deeply, trying to calm his hunger.

She gave him a tentative smile. "How are Aimee and Qadir?"

"Fine, both are fine," he said.

Her hand dropped to the cane. She lifted it and tilted her head in inquiry. He took the cane from her and placed it back against the wall.

"A compromise with my doctor," he replied.

A knock on the door pulled them apart. It was her assistant reminding her of the afterparty she was expected to attend. Idella pursed her lips and her nose scrunched with disdain as she agreed and closed the door. Tarek gave her another lingering kiss.

"I need to shower and change," she said, trailing her hand across his chest.

His eyes blazed with desire as she collected a hanger from the rack, went into the bathroom, and didn't close the door. A gentleman would have looked away when she unfastened the halter top of her dress and the material fell away to reveal lush, round breasts or when she unzipped the lower portion of the dress and let it drop to the floor. Her nude body looked like a painting created by one of the great Masters.

He walked over to the door of the bathroom and leaned against the doorframe. She hung up her gown, stepped into the shower, and smoothed a creamy shower gel over her skin. His eyes followed the movement of the soap bubbles as they slid along her collarbone and down her breasts where they clung for just a brief moment from the dark pebbles of her nipples.

He swallowed. The connection between them was as strong as it had been three years ago, their kiss electric, their passion on a primitive level that defied logic.

"I'm surprised that you came to the show. You should be resting," she said.

His eyes followed the movements of her hands as she slid them over her breasts and down her stomach. Through the clear glass, he could see the tantalizing vee of black curls protecting her womanhood.

"Rest is not what I need right now," he responded.

Her lips curved in a smile. She cupped her breast while her other hand moved between her legs. His hand moved to his cock.

"Come for me," he ordered. "I want to watch you."

Her hand paused for a fraction of a second, their eyes locked in silent challenge, before she obediently began to stroke herself. He groaned. The sensual expression on her face and the way her hips moved with the rhythm of her fingers had him breaking out in a sweat. He placed his hands on the glass and watched her.

Her lips parted on a gasp as she came, her eyes wide and filled with need. A low groan was pulled from Tarek, and their eyes locked again, the connection between them like a live wire.

She turned off the shower with trembling fingers. He pulled the plush cotton towel off the heated towel rack and slid the shower door open. Idella stepped into the towel—and his arms.

Their lips connected again while he ran the towel over her damp skin. He swept his tongue into her mouth, demanding everything, and she gave him that and more. She sucked on his lower lip as if she were caressing his cock.

His whole body pulsed. The sexual tension was beyond anything he had ever experienced before. He felt cool air against his heated flesh and his eyes flew open when Idella's hand wrapped around his cock.

"Let me help you," she murmured against his lips.

She guided him to a chair in the corner of the bathroom. He clenched his hands and his teeth when she pushed his trousers down, unbuttoned his dress shirt and spread it, and then kissed his belly button before she gently pushed him down onto the seat and sank down between his parted thighs. His muscles tightened in response to her erotic caresses.

She slid her soft lips over the head of his cock, and he sucked in a breath, his eyes locked on the arousing image of her tongue sweeping out to taste his pre-cum. A shudder ran through him and he groaned when she took the length of him in her mouth and began pleasuring him.

Her small, taut breasts brushed against his thighs when she slid an arm along his heated skin to caress his taut buttock. Over and over again she stroked him until the tingling that had begun when he was watching her in the shower pulsed through his body like the increasing beat of a drummer. The pressure built to a crescendo before crashing through him in a tsunami that rocked his taut frame.

"Idella... I—" he tried to warn her before he moaned and came in pulsing waves in her mouth.

His breaths came in short pants, and his body trembled from the force of his release. He slid his hand through her hair while her lips squeezed his cock. One of her hands cupped his buttock while the other squeezed his bollocks.

He took in a long, shuddering breath before he pulled her up off her knees and onto his lap where they kissed deeply. He could taste himself on her tongue.

When he finally released her, they stared at each other, not saying a word, yet saying everything. In her slumberous eyes, he saw wonder, fear, and a possessiveness that rivaled his own. She held his gaze and he could almost hear her determined declaration that he was hers and she would take nothing less than everything he had to give.

A voice called through the dressing room door. "Idella, the limousine is ready when you are."

Idella smiled at him. "We'd better get presentable," she said, trailing her fingers along his cock.

Desire flared inside Tarek again. "I'll help you put your gown on—but later, I'll be the one to take it off you," he growled.

"Something to look forward to," Idella purred. She grinned with giddy delight as she looked away.

Twenty minutes later, Tarek escorted Idella toward the waiting limousine. She was wearing a stunning gold gown. Their combined bodyguards kept the throng of fans at a safe distance, but Idella still stopped several times to speak to her excited followers or sign autographs.

He breathed a sigh of relief when they finally slid into the limo. She threaded her fingers through his. This may have been only the second time they had met in person, but he felt like she had been by his side forever.

"We won't have to stay at the reception long. Most people come to these things drunk and only remember that I was even there when they see the tabloid photos tomorrow," she said.

"Good," he replied.

"There is something I should tell you—*before* we are distracted again," she said, turning to look at him with eyes filled with mirth.

He was immediately drawn to her like a moth to a flame. He kissed her, savoring the feeling. She responded with the same heated passion from earlier that had sent them both spiraling out of control.

"What is so important that it cannot wait until later?" he asked.

"I'm still a virgin," she murmured against his lips. She captured his astonished gasp with another kiss.

Five

Idella could feel Tarek's eyes locked on her every movement during the boring party. He had been quiet after her startling announcement in the limo. That might have had something to do with the fact that she could not stop kissing him.

Once they arrived at their destination, it had been a whirlwind of people, music, food, and drink. This wasn't exactly the venue to talk, but she hoped she would still have his company long after they left the party. He had promised to undress her, after all, and she planned to hold him to it.

At twenty-six years of age and with her life experiences, it might seem impossible that she had never been intimate with a man before. The tabloids certainly loved to speculate. The truth was that she had never desired a man the way she desired Tarek, and her years on the streets had shown her the darker side of men.

What she hadn't learned from the men who preyed on her mom, she had learned from Harlem. Control: control of her body, her mind, and her emotions, Harlem had stressed that from the moment he found her in the back alley, crying over her battered mother's corpse.

Even if her lover never turned violent, her enemies could discover her identity and use the people she cared about. She had seen others forget Harlem's lesson—and she'd seen the death and betrayal that had ensued.

"Your songs touch my heart," Harrison MacMillan said.

Idella blinked, tuning back in to the seventy-year-old billionaire who was obviously looking for trophy-wife number five.

"Thank you," she automatically replied.

"I would love to discuss my admiration in a more... private setting," he suggested.

"Idella has a previous commitment," Tarek stated in a hard tone.

Harrison glanced between her and Tarek with an expression of disappointment before he held out his business card. Tarek took the card before she could and pocketed it. Harrison mumbled inaudibly beneath the music before moving away.

"He hadn't gotten to the part where diamonds would look lovely on me," she chuckled.

"He is lucky I didn't cut his hands off. If he tried to touch you one more time...."

She flashed a look to his cane. "Let me guess, you have a sword hidden inside."

He grinned at her. "If I *have* to use this damn thing, it might as well be useful. We've been here almost forty-five minutes. I think it is time to leave."

"Yes, I believe you promised to help me undress."

Their eyes met in an electric moment, and they shared a warm smile before he hastily pulled her through the crowd while she laughed. Anyone who thought to stop their progress quickly changed their mind when he scowled at them. Her body hummed in response to his barely contained desire and the knowledge of what would soon happen between them.

Tarek's driver, Emin, brought them to an elegant house on the outskirts of London. Several members of the paparazzi tried following them, but were delayed by the combined forces of their bodyguards.

They held hands as they climbed the stairs and entered the mansion. He immediately headed for the staircase and by the time they reached his room, they were both breathless.

He closed the door behind him and reached for the zipper of her gown. She kicked off her heels as the gown pooled around her feet, leaving her completely naked. His swiftly inhaled breath drew a sultry smile of invitation to her lips. She looked over her shoulder.

"Did you miss me?" she teased.

He huffed a laugh and pulled his tie free, tossing it to the side. His evening jacket followed.

She turned to face him, walked slowly backwards toward the bed, and crooked her finger at him. His shirt was unbuttoned by the time he reached her.

"You can take care of your shoes and socks. Your pants are mine to remove, though."

He did as she instructed and caught his breath when she sat on the edge of the bed and spread her legs.

This will be worth waiting for, she thought as she bit her lower lip, her eyes glued to the distinctive bulge outlined in his trousers.

Desire could be a dual-edged sword. One side promised pure pleasure and the other the pain of longing and restraint in face of overwhelming excitement. He was definitely feeling an excruciating, erotic pain, and Idella was his commanding mistress.

Her nipples beckoned to him and when she parted her legs, all he could think about was devouring her. He stepped between her thighs, and she pressed her hands against his chest, stopping him from pushing her back.

"Let me explore you... please," she whispered against his lips.

He gave her a brief, jerky nod, unable to trust his voice. At the sensual touch of her fingers sliding across his skin, his eyes partially closed and he gritted his teeth. Time slowed and everything faded but what she was doing to him.

He sucked in his breath when she traced along his waistband before taking her sweet time unbuttoning his pants and sliding the zipper down. He ground his teeth to keep from cursing when cool air caressed his skin as she tugged his trousers and silk black boxers down at the same time. His throbbing cock popped free a hair's breadth from her full lips.

"Idella, *habibi*, please... I don't think—"

"You are so beautiful," she breathed.

A tremor ran through him when her warm breath touched him. His eyes remained locked on her face. The movement of her tongue across her lips, moistening them in preparation, held him mesmerized. He tilted his hips towards her lips, closing the slight distance as need engulfed him.

"Take me," he groaned.

Her lips parted and he slid his cock into her warm mouth. Threading his fingers through her hair, he rocked back and forth as waves of pleasure rose and crashed through his body. The vision of her taking him in her mouth was addictive.

She wrapped one hand around his thick shaft, pumping it while her other hand cupped his engorged bollocks. The slight graze of her teeth along his silken shaft caused him to hiss and shudder. A small amount of pre-cum coated the tip and she ran her tongue along it before swirling around the edge of his bulbous head.

"Sweet sands of the desert... you are going to drive me insane," he moaned.

He pulled back, unable to take any more. Pushing her onto her back on the bed, he dropped to his knees, pulled her legs onto his shoulders, and buried his face against her soft, womanly mound. He attacked her without mercy, licking her until she writhed and begged. Her first orgasm swept over his tongue and her loud scream filled the air.

Thrumming with his own need, he stood and reveled in the view. Her eyes were closed, her lips parted as she gasped for breath, her taut nipples begged to be pinched, and her pussy...

"Slide up the bed and spread your legs wide for me," he ordered in a hoarse voice.

She started to slowly wiggle her way up the length of the bed, but the primitive need to control her slammed into him and he scooped her up in his arms. He laid her back against the pillows and covered her body, caging her beneath him. His eyes remained glued to her face as he wound his fingers around his throbbing shaft. He aligned his cock with her channel and slowly pushed through the soft folds.

She mewled as he impaled her, fisting the bedcovers with her hands and arching her back. He gripped her upper thighs, keeping her stretched wide as he buried himself to the hilt in her. Her muscles squeezed him. Exquisite pain flashed through him and his cock swelled with approval.

"Tarek, please." she moaned, trying to rock against him. "I need you!"

"Come for me, again, Idella. Come for me and I will give you the world."

He began rocking, her sweetness fisting him as if protesting his withdrawal. The tingling at the base of his spine spread outward and he fought against it as he waited for her pleasure to come again. He slid his hands up her sides to her breasts. Thrusting deeply within her, he pinched her nipples. Her hips bucked, her body vibrated, and she released a long gasping cry.

He had never seen anything more beautiful than her face twisted with ecstasy. Her throaty cry of release reverberated through him like a chord on a harp being plucked. The tension built in his body until he felt the fragile thread of his control snap.

Warmth surrounded his cock, her body slick as her orgasm pulsed around him. Tarek relished the sensations and allowed himself to orgasm, the force of his release shocking him. His body jerked as he poured himself into her. His legs trembled and he half collapsed over her.

"We didn't even make... it all the way... under the covers," Idella breathlessly laughed.

A choked laugh of his own escaped him. "Once I have the strength to move, we'll try to make it there," he promised.

"It's okay. You're better than any blanket," she sleepily replied.

He kissed her shoulder. It took several minutes before he was capable of pulling himself free. Idella had fallen asleep. He gently lifted her, tucking her into bed, before he went into the bathroom to clean up. He returned with a warm washcloth and gently cleaned her, too, before climbing in beside her and snuggling close.

He felt intensely possessive in that moment, just like he had earlier. She sighed in her sleep and rolled over, sliding her leg up over his thighs. He held her tightly and smiled as he, too, fell into a deep sleep, entangled with his lover.

They spent the next two days in bed, and it was the most extraordinary time of Tarek's life. On the third day, he was startled awake by the same dream he'd been having every night for the past three weeks.

The details of his near death were much clearer this time—pain searing his side and thigh, the sound of gunfire and his men falling around him, and then the familiar voice of the woman. *"He'll die if I don't."*

The realization hit Tarek so hard that he felt sick to his stomach. It *was* her. Idella and Dallas were the same person. He was remembering, and the evidence was piling up.

He closed his eyes. He had caressed every inch of Idella over the last two days. His fingers had skimmed over scars that she had dismissed as childhood injuries when he asked her about them.

The circular scar that she said resulted from a fall from a tree onto a broken branch, he had seen scars like that before. He had two new ones on his own body—from bullets.

The long mark above her right breast that he had followed with his lips was as thin as a knife's edge. The burn mark on her thigh she claimed came from an errant firework one Fourth of July.

His thoughts were still whirling when Idella returned from the bathroom wearing only his shirt.

"Hi," she said with a flirty smile.

The shirt slipped off her slender shoulder. When he didn't respond right away, she paused in front of him.

"Are you alright?" she asked. She cupped his cheek.

She lied to me. No, maybe she didn't. I don't know that. I could be confused. There could be nothing to this.

The dream had shown Dallas setting down her sniper rifle. He remembered his confusion. An *'amirat khurafiat alsahra'* shouldn't be carrying a sniper rifle.

"We will lose our targets in the mountains if we don't leave now!" Hamlet had argued.

Tarek narrowed his eyes as he thought about that. If their 'targets' were not the royal entourage, that meant Dallas and Hamlet were targeting the Coldhouse brothers—just like he was.

But if we're on the same side, why would she keep this from me?

"Tarek?"

He grabbed her around the waist and rolled so she was beneath him on the bed. She laughed in surprise.

He kissed her smooth shoulder. "Come back to Jawahir with me."

She studied his expression, her own eyes conveying a variety of thoughts as she considered his proposal, and then she kissed him.

"I would love to go to Jawahir with you," she said.

He grinned, and she gave him a brilliant smile in return.

"I'll stop by my hotel, pack, and let my crew know what is going on. Can you send a car for me when you are ready?"

"I could go with you," he suggested.

"If you did that, we'd end up in bed in my hotel room for another two days. I know you have work you need to finish. Pick me up later. That will give me time to rearrange my schedule."

He didn't like the idea of her being out of his sight, but when she caressed his cheek, he kissed the center of her palm and acquiesced.

"I'll be there by four."

"I'll be ready," she promised.

An hour later, he escorted her out of the house and into the limo. As he watched the limo pull away, he gestured to one of his elite body-guards. Emin stepped forward.

"Protect her," he ordered.

"Yes, sire," Emin replied, turning and motioning to the driver of a black SUV.

Tarek returned to the house. The tapping of his cane echoed on the marble floor of the nearly empty mansion. He walked down the hallway to the office. Closing the door, he settled into the large desk chair, placed his cane next to the desk, and opened the computer.

For three hours, he researched Idella. She had shared nothing with him that wasn't public knowledge. He stared at a close-up of her face during one of her live performances. She was wearing a scarf and a veil. Just her eyes were visible, the same eyes that he had seen every night in his dreams since that day in the desert. He pictured her wearing the traditional headgear and throbes of his people, a sniper rifle in her hand, and the images blurred and became one.

His heart tried to reject the connection while his mind sorted and connected missing pieces. What connection was there between Idella and Bronislav? He knew they had never been lovers—but, that didn't mean they didn't have a business arrangement.

Selima suspected that Dallas worked for the American government. Idella's ability to move around the world without raising questions would be beneficial. Anderson Coldhouse was wanted for the murder of a U.S. Marshall who had been protecting Aimee, but would the Americans go to the trouble of sending an assassin after him?

He breathed deeply at the thought. Was Idella a danger to him and his brother? That made little sense either. Dallas could easily have killed him or left him to die in the Black Mountains. Plus, she and the man called Hamlet had later helped in the rescue of Qadir.

Idella being an assassin seemed so implausible. Her hands were soft against his skin. The idea of them being covered in blood was almost impossible for him to imagine. He withdrew his cell phone from his pocket and made a call.

"Jameel, I need you to do me a favor. I want every piece of information you can find on Idella Jones."

"*The* Idella? The singer?"

"Yes," he replied in a curt tone.

"How deep a search are we talking?"

"As deep as you can go."

"Alright. You'll have to give me a couple of days. I may need to reach out to someone who can help."

"Thank you. I'll be home later tonight." He lowered the phone to the desk and walked over to the window to stare out at the gardens. He took another deep breath.

He had *never* felt this way about a woman before, and now....

"Who are you?" he growled in frustration. He lifted his clenched fist and pressed it against the cool glass, lost in his turbulent thoughts.

Six

"Anderson Coldhouse is on the move," Raja said, his voice coming through clearly over the phone. "He's heading back to Jawahir."

"I'm heading there tonight," Idella replied.

"Alone?"

His tense voice told her that he knew she had been with Tarek. The media didn't waste time.

"What better way to keep an eye on the situation than from the inside?" she replied in a light tone.

"I'll stay on Colin and Bronislav," he said. "Does Tarek know about you?"

"No," she replied in a barely audible voice.

If Harlem were alive and knew of the situation, he would have put a bullet between Tarek's eyes and told her the problem was solved. But she was free of Harlem now. No more chains.

She still didn't want Tarek to know, though. Not yet. Perhaps not ever.

There was a pause on Raja's end. "You'll know when the time is right —if it ever is," he said, as if reading her mind.

"I'll see you soon," she replied, ending the call.

Idella stared out the window of her London hotel room, deep in thought. Even if things turned serious between herself and Tarek, she might not have to confess. She hoped this would be her final mission.

The Coldhouse brothers had failed to start a war between Simdan and Jawahir, and they had failed to kill Sheikh Qadir or extract the state secrets they wanted from him. The Coldhouse brothers and Bronislav shouldn't be underestimated—they were certainly well-protected weasels, popping up and disappearing just as quickly—but there was every chance that this mission to take them down wouldn't last much longer. Aimee had resurfaced, and she would be perceived as the weak link in Qadir's armor.

Colin had flown out to debrief Bronislav. The one recent success Colin could boast about was breaking Rashid al Hamid out of prison. Rashid would be their political puppet—or their fall-guy, depending on how well their plans panned out. At this stage of the operation, it was unlikely that Colin would be replaced, no matter how many failures he'd had. Colin was an experienced killer and an expert in getting unsavory things done. It was Anderson who was the loose cannon, and Bronislav was smart enough to see that.

Anderson had a tendency to lose sight of the mission while he pursued personal matters like petty revenge, and Colin didn't enjoy looking like a fool. The two brothers had a turbulent relationship at the best of times. Colin had bailed his younger brother out of trouble a dozen times and sealed the records, but Anderson was a clinically diagnosed sociopath. His impulsive, violent behavior and selfishness was unlikely to ever change.

Eventually, Colin was going to stop tolerating Anderson as a liability. In the meantime, Anderson would continue to do damage to his opposition *and* his own side. It would probably be Anderson that they would take down first. Colin might even shove him into their path and wash his hands of his brother once and for all.

Or maybe not, she thought with a rueful laugh. *The bonds of family are tough to unravel.*

Idella frowned as she finished packing and automatically wiped the room down thoroughly to remove any fingerprints. A glance at the clock informed her it was almost four o'clock.

All of her performance gowns were taken care of by her team, so she was able to pack light. She slung her designer travel bag over her shoulder, wrapped a white scarf around her hair, and checked her outfit. She was wearing a loose white, button-up blouse with a white silky camisole under it, a pair of light faded jeans with tears across the thighs, and white trainers.

She scanned the room one more time, slid on a pair of sunglasses, and exited the room. Her heart pounded with anticipation, and soon she was walking toward Tarek as he emerged from his limousine. His security team moved like a well-oiled machine with him at the center. Idella took them all in with a glance before she focused on the man who made her heart swell.

"Hi, stranger," she greeted Tarek with a brilliant smile.

For a brief moment, his unsmiling expression made her feel uncertain, but then his shoulders relaxed and he returned her smile. She moved into his arms just as a photographer appeared from behind one of the hotel's decorative columns.

"Retrieve his camera," Tarek ordered two of his guards.

Idella rested her hand on his arm. "Wait."

Tarek signaled his guards to do as she asked, and a moment later, she was posing with the photographer, making goofy faces, and laughing. Tarek's dark scowl made it even funnier.

Walking past him, she gave him a cheeky smile. "The best way to deal with them is to fight fire with fire. I deleted the photos of us together when I was looking at the photos of him with me. When he gets home, he'll realize those are the only ones he has."

Tarek's lips curved into a reluctant smile. "That is one way to do it, I suppose."

"Oh, you wish you had thought of it," she laughed, climbing into the back of the limo.

The moment Adel shut the door, she turned and wrapped her arms around Tarek. He pressed her close and captured her lips in a lingering kiss. She arched into him and sighed with pleasure.

"I missed you," he murmured, his eyes burning with intensity.

"You can show me how much later," she flirted, biting her lip. "I've never been to the capital city of Jawahir. You'll have to tell me about it. My first question is: is it warm? I'm ready for a little sunshine and warmth."

Tarek narrowed his eyes. "You said 'the capital city'. Have you visited other places in Jawahir?"

"I've traveled a lot, but I haven't been *everywhere*." she laughed, threading her fingers through his. "Tell me about your country. I want to hear you describe it in your own words."

Tarek tried not to notice that Idella's answer could be construed as evasive. Perhaps she meant it as a simple 'no' or perhaps she intended to mislead him. Staring into her eyes, he saw no deception in their depths. Her excitement and curiosity seemed genuine, and once again, he was torn by doubt.

"Jawahir is beautiful. To the north, we have the Aljibal Alsawda', or Black Mountains. They span the border with Simdan and continue to the western deserts. To the east are the shimmering turquoise waters of the Arabian Sea. To the south are the plateaus where most of our gems are mined. There is a great amount of diversity within each region, and they are all very significant in our country's history."

"Which is your favorite?"

He paused. "The east. I would love to take you to one of the small islands near the coast. We can be alone there."

"I love the water." She caressed the front of his pants while she looked up at him impishly.

Heat flared through him and his breath caught in his throat.

"You don't act like an innocent," he laughed.

She chuckled. The sound was soft and seductive. He wondered if Sirens were real, because everything about Idella drove him mad with desire.

"I read a lot," she replied, "—and I've been on one too many tour buses with young people. I can't avert my eyes every time!"

His eyes twinkled and he pressed her hand against the hard evidence of his attraction to her.

"Perhaps you can share some of what you saw."

She grinned. "There are a few things I might be curious to try…."

Tarek captured her lips, she threaded her fingers between the buttons of his shirt to touch his chest—and then his cell phone vibrated. He reluctantly broke their kiss.

She darted in for one last kiss and touched her tongue to his lips, causing him to feel another surge of heat before she sat back in her seat with a pleased expression. Her lips were wet and swollen and very distracting.

He retrieved his phone from the pocket of his jacket and answered it without looking at the caller ID, his eyes never leaving Idella as she pulled a compact mirror out of her purse and touched up her lips with a clear gloss.

"Tarek," he answered.

"I was beginning to wonder if you were going to answer. Is she there with you?" Jameel asked.

"Yes," he replied, settling back in his seat.

"Meet me after you get settled."

As Tarek agreed to something with whoever he was talking to, Idella adjusted her headscarf and rubbed a spot on her cheek. Her own phone chimed with a text message—from Bugs. She smiled even as her heart thundered in her chest.

> Be careful. Jam-man is researching you. How much do you want him to know?

She quickly texted back.

> Only public info. Deflect his search. Keep me advised. Please.

Tarek ended his phone call, and she cheerfully asked, "Is everything alright?"

"Yes… and you?" he asked, nodding to her phone.

"Nothing to worry about," she replied.

The limo slowed as it went through security at the private entrance to the airport. A glance out the window showed a Boeing 747-8 VIP jet was waiting for them.

She placed her bag on the floor and gave him what she hoped was a sexy look as she carefully rebuttoned the three buttons she had undone. His surprised chuckle told her he hadn't even been aware that she had begun to undress him.

"You are a very dangerous woman," he replied.

"You have no idea," she softly confessed.

Seven

Nasir, Jawahir

Capital city

Anderson Coldhouse slowly wiped the rag over the Sig Sauer M17 9mm Luger and ignored the three men at the kitchen table who were quietly playing their game of cards.

His mind wandered, and his fingers flexed as he simmered in a familiar rage. Colin was in Moscow with Bronislav, answering for their failure to start a war between Simdan and Jawahir.

It wasn't Anderson's fault. It was that bitch Aimee Wheels' fault. She was supposed to be dead. His hand shook, and he clenched his fist.

His cell phone lit up. It was Colin. He reached for it, answering it on the second ring.

"What happened?" he demanded.

"I have a job for you," Colin said, his voice cold.

Anderson had a sudden desire to empty his gun into the men at the table. Bran, the perceptive bastard, openly stared at him. Anderson stared back.

"What is it?" he replied as he brought his clean side-arm into the bedroom. He used the tip of his gun to draw back the window's sheer curtain and peered into the alley.

"Capture Aimee Wheels and bring her to me."

"Capture…. Why not just kill her?"

Colin vehemently cursed Anderson's name. It brought up memories of his brother beating him. He tapped his temple with the tip of his gun as he tried to drive the memories away.

"Don't *fucking* screw this up, Anderson. I need her alive. If you don't get it done this time, Bronislav wants you dead. I'm serious. Get me the Wheels woman—alive. I'll send Bran the route to get her out of the country. You've got three experienced men with you. Don't fuck up this time," Colin ordered.

"I'll get her."

He hung up and put the phone in his pocket, moodily staring out the window. His brother was sending the information to Bran—not him. Colin didn't trust him.

Get the girl, get out, and everything will be alright.

He repeated the chant over and over until he felt his mind calm. He would get the girl, get out, and kill Bran. Then his brother would have to depend on him.

Idella's eyes were now hidden behind a pair of fashion-designer sunglasses, and she had pulled a sheer, gold scarf from her bag, wrapped it around her hair, and tied it under her chin.

Her movements were so elegant and feminine that once again Tarek doubted that she could have been the woman on the mountain. Everything about her screamed 'fragile'.

"The flight will be approximately six hours. We can dine first or later," he said.

She smiled. "Later. I'd like to… 'rest' for a bit," she replied with a flirty glance.

On impulse, he removed her sunglasses. He wanted to see her eyes. She looked startled for a moment before she plucked her sunglasses from his hand and placed them in the front pocket of her bag, her hazel eyes amused and affectionate.

As the plane pulled out of the hanger, he held her hand, she sipped her fruit juice, and within minutes, the jet was soaring into the dreary London skies. They reached their intended altitude, and Tarek unfastened his seatbelt, rose to his feet, and held out his hand.

"Mile high club," she murmured with a shy smile as she placed her hand in his. "Another first for me."

He brought her close and wrapped his arm around her waist.

"I hope to give you many more," he replied.

Tarek pulled on the pair of black silk boxers and loose-fitting black trousers that he would wear under his throbe. When he was home, he tended to dress in the more traditional style. It made more sense in the heat. As Idella dried her lithe body, he traced a scar on her back. It looked fresh, maybe a month old.

"What happened?" he asked.

She chuckled and caressed his bare stomach. He sucked in a breath.

"Are you going to ask me that every time I get a new bump, cut, or bruise? If so, it will be a full-time job kissing my boo-boos."

She looked over her shoulder at him before she retrieved fresh clothes from the cabin. The bra, long-sleeve blouse, linen slacks, and lace thong were all white. She slid on the skimpy underwear, and the thin strip between her legs teased him as she bent over to pull her slacks on.

He breathed out and shook his head at her. "I can't think straight when you are…." He waved his hand at her.

She walked over to him, dangling her bra by a long, slender finger, and slowly caressed down his chest before she lightly touched the wound in his side.

"I'm fine," he assured her with a scowl.

Her eyes darkened, the green highlights in her hazel eyes deepening. "Sex is a great workout, but like anything, it needs to be… balanced. You are still recovering from being shot."

He grabbed her hand and pulled it to his lips. "We don't have sex. We make love," he retorted, nipping the tips of her fingers.

She caught her breath and leaned into him. The tips of her breasts teased his bare chest. She moaned, and he slid his hands up along her back, enjoying her shiver of response. They were explosive together. He had never wanted a woman as much as he wanted Idella.

"I would love to live on our lovemaking alone, but if I don't get some sustenance I won't have the energy," she teased.

Tarek kissed her quickly and released her. He paused as he realized that, once again, she had deflected his questions.

Ten minutes later, the steward delivered an exquisite dinner for each of them—lobster, pilaf rice, and steamed asparagus for him while she had baked chicken with a side salad. They each enjoyed a glass of Chardonnay.

They talked about Jawahir, about her latest tour, about the politics of the world, but all the while he studied her and thought about his unanswered questions. He waited until the steward refilled their glasses and removed their empty plates.

"There was a woman on the mountain where I was shot. She had eyes like yours," he began.

Idella smiled. "Really? I would say that is fascinating, but my eyes aren't that unusual."

His eyes locked with hers as she lifted her wine glass to her lips.

"They are, actually. Your eyes are beautiful... and very distinctive. Her voice was just like yours, too," he continued.

Her eyes grew serious. "You were shot, Tarek. A traumatic injury with significant blood loss can cause your mind to do strange things. Don't you think it is possible—and more probable—that you transferred the memory of meeting me to the woman you saw when you were injured?"

"I would agree except for one important factor," he conceded, his eyes still trained on her face.

She raised an eyebrow.

"My reaction to her was the same I have to you," he replied.

The steward walked over and politely advised them to fasten their seatbelts for landing, collecting their empty wine glasses while the captain's voice came over the intercom system to give an update on their impending arrival. Idella collected her scarf and put on her sunglasses, concealing her eyes.

"This conversation is not finished," he announced as the plane began its descent.

A slight smile curved her lips. "I never thought to ask how you usually handle bringing your mistresses home. Where will I be staying? Will your family know about me?"

A flash of anger swept through him before he tamped it down. "You are not my mistress and my family will be honored to meet you," he stated.

"If I'm not your mistress, then what am I?" she curiously asked.

"More," he answered without looking at her. "Much more."

He could feel her eyes on him as the plane's wheels touched down and the captain informed them about the time and temperature.

Soon it was time to deplane, and Tarek offered his hand to her. She accepted, squeezing his hand as she rose from her seat.

"Welcome to Jawahir," he said as he guided her to the exit.

Eight

Idella stood at the window in the airy sitting room of an apartment that belonged to a friend of Tarek's. It was a place he visited often when he needed a break from palace life.

Raja had delivered an untraceable SSG 69 sniper rifle and additional gear to the apartment. How he had known about the place before she did, she didn't bother asking. The case and other items she would need were tucked behind a new access panel in the guest bedroom closet just like Raja said they would be.

The palace could be seen in the distance, but Idella was too embroiled in her thoughts to look at it. Her lies and emotional manipulation were weighing on her.

It had taken a considerable effort to persuade Tarek to let her stay here instead of with his family. She could not tell him that it would not be helpful to her mission for everyone, including Anderson Coldhouse and Aimee Wheels, to know she was in Jawahir.

Instead, she had pointed out that they should keep things private until they knew where their relationship was going. While Jawahir was more progressive than many other Middle Eastern countries, it was still conservative.

When that didn't work, she had pleaded her need for privacy as she adjusted to having a lover for the first time. Despite his assurances that the palace staff would say nothing, she reminded him of the recent tabloid articles on other royal couples and the strain it had placed on their relationships.

She had refused to budge, and Tarek grudgingly admitted that he understood. After she reluctantly accepted Emin and Dhamar as her bodyguards, they settled into the apartment and fell into a pattern where Tarek split his time between the palace and the apartment while she attended to work or explored the city.

She remembered everything Bugs and Raja had found out about Tarek's team, and it was very useful information now that she would be seeing them more often. Emin was the guard who had followed her from Tarek's London residence to her hotel—Emin al Fadil. Thirty-two years old, never married, he entered the military at seventeen by lying about his age, he was six feet tall, weighed one hundred and eighty pounds, and he was lethal in several forms of martial arts. He was an expert with most weapons, his favorite being the M4/M4A1 Carbine.

Dhamar Elga was devilishly handsome with the best features of his Jawahiran father and his Italian mother. The second-born son of his family, he had left home to get away from the pressure to marry. He was thirty years old, was fluent in eight languages, had enough medical training to be a doctor, and he enjoyed the ladies.

The other two guards, the ones who were sticking close to Tarek, were Adel and Butrus. Adel Aslam was the son of a tribal sheikh. He'd been married and widowed before he was twenty. It was an arranged marriage, and it had not been pleasant. His wife had died while enjoying a tryst in France. Adel had received extensive sniper training in the United Kingdom. He was twenty-nine years old, he served in the military with Tarek, and he was an expert marksman.

Butrus Djendib was the one Idella would be the most cautious around. He had a genius IQ. He was also a blood-hound, having grown up on the streets of Simdan. Very little was known about his family. The youngest on the team, he was twenty-seven years old, and when he enlisted in the military, there was a long string of disciplinary issues before Tarek picked him to be on his team. It was with Tarek that Butrus's formidable talents blossomed.

The four men were lucky to be alive. Normally they would have been with Tarek and Qadir in the convoy when it was attacked, but Tarek had temporarily assigned the guards to his parents after a serious threat was uncovered against the elder royal couple.

The King and Queen's personal guards were injured in a suspicious 'accident'. Colin Coldhouse and Bronislav had planned the distraction hoping Tarek would do exactly what he did—separate from the guards who could protect the heir and his brother best.

When word reached them about the attack on Qadir and Tarek's convoy, the team would have died before they ever arrived at the scene. Bugs intercepted a message describing a plot to sabotage the helicopter normally used by the team. Idella had passed the information to Butrus via an anonymous tip.

Now she wished she had passed it to Dhamar. Butrus was continuing to dig into where the tip had come from—almost a month after the incident—and he wasn't the only one.

She could handle whatever they threw at her. She did feel slightly ridiculous about hiding her secret when she could easily tell Tarek the truth, but... she wasn't ready to tell him, that was all there was to it. Maybe when she felt certain he could handle every side of her... no. No, she'd only tell him if she was left with no other choice. He cared for her singer persona. It was better to not rock the boat.

She checked in daily with Raja. Their most recent encrypted conversation had been short but to the point. Anderson Coldhouse was in Nasir.

Idella's phone vibrated. A digital bug scrambled across her screen and a message popped up.

> Aimee and Selima heading out to market
> again.

Bugs sent her a map with Anderson Coldhouse's movements, and Idella bit back a curse.

"Emin, I'm going to be working on some new songs with my team," she called out.

Emin moved to the doorway of the security suite. "I'll make sure that I don't disturb you," he promised.

"Thank you. I'll probably be exhausted afterwards, so if you don't hear anything, it means I'm passed out."

Emin smiled. "I enjoy listening to your creativity," he admitted.

Idella laughed. "I'm glad I can make babysitting me a little entertaining."

"It is an honor to guard you," Emin replied with a bow of his head.

Idella smiled in return and turned away. This would be the second time she slipped out without them realizing she was gone. She glanced over her shoulder and saw that Emin had partially closed the en-suite security office door.

She headed to the office area and inserted a recording of one of her studio sessions. It would sound like she was on speaker phone with her studio producer and musicians back home. A microphone system would allow her to hear if anyone tried to enter the office so she could respond as if she were in the room.

Once it was set up, she peered out of the room, and then locked it behind her as she crept to the guest bedroom closet. She covered her clothing with a traditional male throbe and headdress, retrieved the equipment Raja had left her, and silently exited the apartment via the service entrance.

She knew Dhamar was downstairs in the lobby. To avoid him, she took the stairwell down to the fifteenth floor, then caught the west wing's elevator, and finally walked out a side door with neither of her guards the wiser.

Idella smiled as she watched Aimee and Selima browse in the market. Aimee's enthusiasm was one of the things Idella had always loved about her. Wheels was one of the few people in the world who could see the ugliness of human nature and still remain virtually untouched by it.

Of course, Idella helped that happen however she could. After Dallas's late-night visit with Biggy—the local gang leader in Harlem—the young man had understood that he was *not* the big fish around here and she would hold him personally responsible if anything happened to the two ladies under her protection: Midnight and Wheels.

Selima was busy bargaining with a vendor over a colorful scarf when Aimee moved to a different stall and lifted her phone to her ear. Idella's own phone vibrated. She glanced down and read the message.

> Aimee receiving following call:

Anderson Coldhouse's voice came through her earpiece. *"Didn't Agent Hartley warn you to never return to your past?"*

Idella tightened her grip on the strap of her case. Her gaze flickered to another text message on her phone.

> I've traced Anderson's phone. Pushing through real-time tracking.

Anderson was within striking distance. Unfortunately, he was also on the move and Bugs was unable to get a fix on him in the crowded marketplace. Idella calculated she had less than ten minutes to get to the central market. There was no doubt in her mind that Aimee would not only go where Anderson ordered her to go, but she would lose Selima and her bodyguards. Idella needed to stay one step ahead of them.

Nine

"Keep Aimee in your sights and let me know what is happening while I get into position," Tarek ordered Qadir and their guards before he took off for the marine patrol boat.

Butrus had spotted the marine patrol from his vantage point and alerted him that it was about to dock a short distance up the river. Tarek's gut was telling him that Coldhouse was going to grab Aimee and escape to international waters. They needed to have coverage on land, water, and air without alerting Coldhouse to their presence. If Coldhouse knew, he could easily kill Aimee and disappear.

Adel would soon have Coldhouse in his sights and would put a bullet between the man's eyes at the first opportunity. Qadir had skillfully passed Aimee a communication earpiece as she headed to the spot Anderson demanded she go. While it wasn't ideal that Aimee was determined to walk into the lion's mouth, they *did* want to catch that lion and make him talk.

Tarek kept tabs on Qadir's conversation with Aimee as he hurried toward the water's access point. Sweat ran down the collar of his shirt and his leg protested the exertion, but days of physical therapy and his own intense workouts were paying off. Qadir was walking her through how she would survive this.

"Whatever happens, do not let Coldhouse take you."

"He threatened to kill more of my friends, Qadir. The Yangs—" Aimee's voice shook with emotion.

Tarek's heart hurt for Aimee and he replied before Qadir could, "They are fine, Aimee."

"I saw the pictures. Anderson said—"

"The images were fake. I asked the FBI to verify the information." He reassured her that Anderson Coldhouse did not have nearly the same power that he did when he targeted her three years ago. The NYPD had purged their rogue officers and was still monitored by the U.S. Department of Justice to this day.

"You're positive?" Aimee asked in a barely audible voice.

Qadir answered her just as Tarek arrived at his destination. The patrol boat's engine was running. One Marine Officer held the bow rope while the other kept the boat firmly against the concrete retaining wall. Their eyes widened when they saw Tarek.

"Your Highness!" the officer holding the rope exclaimed with surprise.

Tarek stepped past the man and onto the boat. "I need your assistance. We're looking for a sleek, fast boat with at least two men on board. They will be heavily armed."

"We've seen several boats like that today. Do you have a description of the boat?" the driver inquired.

"No, but they should be in the vicinity of the bridge," he responded in frustration.

The officers took their places as Tarek shielded his eyes against the brilliant sunshine and looked over the sparkling water. Dozens of water crafts ranging from luxurious yachts to small pleasure crafts dotted the inlet. He was frustrated that he didn't have more information, and right on cue, Qadir's voice came through his earpiece, asking if he had found them yet.

"We are working on it," he replied.

He noticed a particular boat at the same time Selima warned that it was heading toward Aimee. It was a high-powered speed boat, the colors dark red and black.

Tarek pointed, and his driver moved them closer. The officer who wasn't driving took up a spot near the bow of the boat with his side arm at the ready.

Qadir spoke again, his voice strained and urgent. "Tarek—"

"I see it. Two men in the boat. I don't have a clear shot yet."

A brief glance behind showed that a sailboat was creeping forward at a snail's pace, blocking Adel's shot. Tarek looked forward in time to see a man under the bridge grab Aimee.

He cursed when the boat pulled away with Aimee and Anderson on board. He cursed louder when Qadir launched himself after them, vaulting over the widening gap between the boat and the retaining wall.

Qadir landed in the boat, slamming into one of the men on board. The blow knocked the man back, and as the driver sped up, the man tumbled overboard. The boat fishtailed. The jerking movement of the vessel knocked Qadir out of the path of a bullet.

Anderson aimed again, and the stern of the speedboat almost collided with the retaining wall. An intense struggle broke out as Aimee fought with Anderson.

Tarek's heart thundered when the driver twisted in his seat and aimed his gun at Qadir.

"Shoot the driver, Adel! Shoot the driver!" Tarek shouted, forgetting for a moment that if Adel had a clear shot, he would have already killed them all. Qadir was going to die, and Tarek could do nothing.

The gunman's head suddenly jerked back and a hole appeared in the center of his forehead. Tarek's relief was short-lived. The weight of the dead man pressed the throttle forward and the boat sped toward the retaining wall on the far side of the inlet.

"That wasn't me," Adel said with surprise.

Confusion creased Tarek's brow, but he didn't have time to contemplate who could have taken the shot. Aimee and Qadir jumped in the water seconds before the boat impacted with the concrete wall and exploded.

Tarek's driver slowed the patrol boat, and they carefully searched the water for their Crown Prince and the woman who would one day be their Queen.

Ten

Smoke billowed from the destroyed speedboat. On the roof of the ten-story business building, Idella looked through her scope, searching the area thoroughly, including up and down along the retaining wall. Aimee and Qadir had been pulled to safety, but Anderson and one of his accomplices had also jumped in the water before the boat crashed, and they hadn't been found yet.

Her cell phone vibrated. Pulling it free of her vest, Idella interrupted her recording at home and activated the microphone to relay her voice into the office at the apartment. She forced a smile to her lips as she answered the phone.

"Hello, love. What's up?"

"Are you alright?" Tarek asked, his voice warm and low. Idella's eyes widened slightly and she gave a half smile. Aimee was targeted because of how much Qadir cared for her, which clearly led Tarek to believe Idella would be targeted as well.

"I'm fine. What's all the commotion in the background?" she asked, glancing at Aimee being loaded into an ambulance.

"Nothing to worry about, but I'll be back to the apartment later than I expected tonight."

She smiled at the domesticity of that, her stomach filling with butterflies at the thought of him coming home to her. They wrapped up the call, Idella resumed the recording of her working in the office, and she pocketed her cell phone. A flash of light caught her attention and she swung her scope to focus on the spot.

A curse slipped from her when she noticed Adel staring up at her. She quickly gathered her equipment, swept the area, and made her escape, slipping into a utility room to break down her rifle, change into her civilian-wear, and stash her black clothing, rifle, and other equipment into the oversized beige tote she had brought.

She carefully tucked her hair under the royal blue scarf, covered the lower half of her face, and added a pair of cheap sunglasses. Her outfit was a royal blue tunic, long skirt, and white ballerina flats. She had no sooner stepped out of the room and into the corridor when several men in uniform converged on the landing from the stairwell.

She stepped to the side, bowing her head, as they rushed by her. The elevator pinged ahead of her and she stepped inside and turned. She gripped the tote when a familiar figure paused at the end of the corridor and looked at her with an intense frown.

The elevator doors closed, blocking Butrus's penetrating glare, and Idella breathed a sigh of relief. She pulled out her cell phone and quickly typed a message to Bugs. Once she received confirmation, she leaned back against the wall of the elevator. Bugs would wipe all the security cameras in the building and within a four-block radius. If she was lucky, her mistake wouldn't lead to her getting caught just yet.

She pressed the button for several floors, and moved to the left when two women entered the elevator. One of them had a silver scarf trailing out of her purse.

Idella discretely pulled the scarf free. When the elevator doors opened on the second floor, she stepped out with a soft murmur, and found the women's bathroom. Once inside, she pulled her tunic off and turned it inside out, allowing the silver lining to be the exterior of her new outfit when she put the shirt back on. She pulled the royal blue headscarf off her head and replaced it with the silver one, making sure all of her hair was tucked in. She attached the blue scarf to her bag as a decorative bow.

There wasn't a lot more she could do. She hoped it would be enough. She stepped out of the bathroom and made her way to the staircase.

On the ground floor, several members of Tarek's elite team stood at the entrance. She waited inside the stairwell until a group of five women disembarked from the elevator. She fell into step with them. Each of them murmured a nervous greeting to the men as they passed by.

Idella stepped outside onto the sidewalk, and released her breath as she turned away from the excitement downtown. She needed to update Raja. Until there was concrete proof—as in his dead body—she would proceed as if Anderson had survived.

"No sign of Coldhouse's body. The search is still on," Adel stated.

It was a little after eight that night in Tarek's office. Both Adel and Butrus wore grim expressions. Tarek waved for them to settle into the chairs in front of his ornately carved mahogany desk with a weary hand.

Adel's expression was earnest as he sat and leaned forward, his elbows resting on his knees. Butrus was thoughtful as he sprawled in his chair, stretching his long legs out in front of him.

"The merc pulled from the water isn't talking... yet," Butrus added.

The room fell quiet, but Tarek didn't miss the pointed look that Butrus shot Adel nor the raised eyebrow he got in return. Irritated by the two men's uncharacteristic reluctance to speak their minds, he folded his arms and waited.

"I didn't shoot the driver," Adel finally said. "I never had a clear shot."

Tarek frowned over this puzzle, trying to think of someone besides his mystery woman who would help his family without identifying themselves. It had to be her, didn't it? And not just because he was obsessed with her.

"There was a sniper on the Business Center Building two blocks from the river. The shot was taken from the rooftop. It was a clean shot, center of the forehead," Adel informed him.

Tarek steepled his fingers under his chin, listening intently.

"I saw the driver's head snap back, counted the seconds until I heard the reverb and gauged where it had come from. I glimpsed the shooter on the roof. Whoever it was, they were searching the river for survivors. We didn't get there in time to thank the shooter. They left in such a hurry," Adel sardonically continued.

"Do you think it was one of Coldhouse's men? A Cleaner to silence the survivors?" Tarek asked.

Adel and Butrus both shook their heads.

"No," Adel shared in a low, worried voice. "When we fished out one of the accomplices alive, there was plenty of time and opportunity for the shooter to take him out when he was hauled to shore. They also could have taken out you, Tarek, and Aimee at any point."

The quiet settled again with Adel and Butrus glancing at each other. Adel's expression displayed his unease. Butrus was as stone-faced as ever, but his breathing was slightly elevated. Tarek narrowed his eyes. Butrus never huffed and puffed.

"Do you have any theories?" he asked.

"I think it was a woman," Butrus said, not looking Tarek in the eye.

He stiffened. "How do you know?"

Butrus growled, sat forward, and ran his hands through his hair. He looked as frustrated as Tarek felt at the moment. Butrus rose to his feet and began pacing.

"I *think* it was a woman. My gut *tells* me it was a woman," Butrus grumbled, dropping his hands to his side. "We reached the top floor. We were heading to the roof. There was a woman in the corridor. She was tall, slender... very... elegant. She stepped aside, bowed her head as we passed, and then headed to the elevator. There was something... I could sense.... There was something," Butrus growled, turning to look at Adel with an accusing expression before he turned his attention to Tarek.

"What could you sense?"

"Danger. She stared back at me as the elevator doors closed and I knew... I knew I was looking at a person who could kill me before I even knew death was coming. I know this sounds weird, but when you've lived like I have... you know."

Tarek believed him. He had never in his life seen Butrus shaken like he was now. For a woman to do that—

"Did you recognize her?" he asked.

Butrus shook his head. "No. Her face was covered. There was nothing to identify her except what I described. I contacted the guards at each exit. No one wearing her outfit left the building. Hell, I don't know how she could have gotten a damn *sniper rifle* past any of us!"

"Before you ask," Adel added, "I've had Abdal check all the security cameras within a four-block radius. Nothing. The building's security camera system was wiped for one hour before and one hour after. Whoever was there was a professional with a lot of clout and backup."

Tall, slender, elegant.... Butrus's words played like a broken record through Tarek's mind.

Yet, he had spoken to Idella. He had called Dhamar and Emin as well. They both swore that Idella was doing exactly what she said she was— working on new songs.

He swallowed as he remembered the woman's voice from the mountain and her eyes flashed through his mind. He felt like he was going crazy. All records indicated that when he was attacked, Idella was on the other side of the world, not in Jawahir.

"I want a full autopsy on Anderson's driver. Find Coldhouse's body, give a full description of the woman to Abdal, and spread the security camera search out ten blocks in every direction," Tarek ordered.

"Yes, sir," Adel and Butrus both replied.

It was a few minutes before midnight when Tarek joined his father in the family sitting room. His eyes burned, his head hurt, and his leg was throbbing. He walked over to the bar and poured himself a drink.

"I would suggest you return to that apartment you are staying in and get some much-needed rest, but I know you would ignore me," his father reflected with wry humor.

Tarek looked at his father before he lifted the glass to his lips. King Melik was surprisingly aware of more than his sons wanted to share. Forty years ruling a country provided a long time to build a network of information.

"You're right. I would ignore you," he replied with a grin to ease the words.

"She is exquisite, by the way… and talented. I have most of her songs," Melik commented.

Tarek really didn't want to have this conversation. In all honesty, he didn't know what to say about Idella. He needed to clear his head of the visions and memories plaguing him—and find out what was the truth.

"She is, on both counts," he finally answered.

He focused on his drink. The intense stare his father was giving him reminded him of the times he and his brothers had gotten into trouble.

"She would be a good match for you," his father added before the door opened and Qadir entered.

He breathed a sigh of relief that the conversation would veer away from his personal life. There was still a lot to discuss before he could return to the apartment. Tomorrow, he would have a talk with Emin and Dhamar—and review the personal security equipment he had set up unbeknownst to anyone else.

Eleven

Idella silently watched Tarek enter their bedroom a little after two in the morning. She rolled onto her side, and when he exited the bathroom a short time later, her gaze followed him in the dim light. Her heart did that little dance it did whenever she saw him.

"I missed you today," she murmured.

He stopped, and she pulled the covers back for him. He pulled the towel from his waist and tossed it onto a chair. Her breath caught. When he climbed into bed, she curled up against his side and slid her hand down along his hip.

"I didn't mean to wake you," he said, wrapping his arms around her.

She tilted her head back and kissed him. "You didn't. I took a nap earlier," she said.

His arms tightened around her as she tenderly stroked his hip. She wasn't trying to arouse him. After the long day, she knew he had to be exhausted, but when she did feel his arousal, she raised up far enough to slide her leg over him, and straddled his waist.

"You are beautiful," he murmured, reaching up to cup her breasts.

She chuckled. "I promised myself that I was going to let you rest tonight."

His hands skimmed down to her hips. "I will sleep much better if I'm thoroughly relaxed," he promised.

She rose far enough to align his cock with her ready core. They both moaned when Tarek's velvety head penetrated her. She slowly began to ride him. Tonight was about love and she poured every ounce of her love for Tarek into this intimate dance. She watched his face as she moved, loving every change as they caressed each other.

Neither of them spoke. Instead, they used their hands and lips. A low, moaning cry broke from her when she climaxed. Tarek thrust as deep as he could go as she pulsed around him. His face showed his strain.

She was still coming down from the heights she had reached when he suddenly pulled out of her and rolled her over, pulling her up onto her hands and knees. Gone was the tender lover, and in his place was a man who wanted to claim her.

Her fingers tightened in the sheets as he impaled her. He gripped her hips, thrusting hard and fast. They panted desperately as the tension in both of them built. Idella didn't think she could come again after her first explosive orgasm. When she did, it was unexpected and intense. Her mewling cry shattered the quiet.

"Yes... yes... y-es," Tarek groaned, leaning over her.

He slid his arms around her waist, holding them together as he lowered them to the bed. Idella's eyes burned with emotion from the intensity of their lovemaking and fear engulfed her at the thought of anything ever happening to him.

"Never let me go," she whispered, closing her eyes as a tear slid down her face.

"Never, *habibi*. I will never let you go," he promised.

She remained awake long after Tarek's breathing deepened in exhausted slumber. Slipping from the bed, she went into the bathroom and cleaned up. She retrieved her cell phone and sent a message to Raja and to Bugs. She needed to find Anderson Coldhouse before he could strike again.

Early the next morning, Idella sipped a cup of coffee and stared out the window. Soft footsteps warned her that Tarek was approaching. He paused in the entranceway to the living room. She could feel his eyes on her. '

She turned with a smile. "Good morning," she greeted.

He studied her with an unsmiling face. She felt uncertain, a rare feeling for her, and her smile faltered.

She tilted her head in inquiry. He walked forward and placed a flash drive on the table. Her wary gaze moved from the memory stick to his face.

"I need you to be honest with me before I look at this," he said.

Her eyes narrowed at his tone. "Perhaps you should explain why I should be concerned."

He stepped away from the table and poured himself a cup of coffee. She could feel the tension radiating off of him. Her eyes moved to the memory stick again.

"Ever since I was wounded, I've been having dreams about the woman on the mountain—the woman who saved my life even though it wasn't part of her mission," he said.

"It isn't uncommon to have flashbacks. Dreams can often be a mixture of real events and unrelated memories," she replied in a cautious tone.

He turned to face her. "I remember what happened on that mountain before I was knocked unconscious," he stated in a hard voice.

She lifted her chin. "Does it really matter?"

"It does to me, because I think I know who she is," Tarek quietly replied.

Her eyes followed his to the flash drive. Tears burned the back of her eyes. She tried to push the sense of betrayal away, knowing it was stupid to feel let down when she was the one who had been lying. She fingered the memory stick.

"You set up recording equipment inside the apartment," she guessed.

"Yes, and other places," he replied.

"Not attached to the Internet so they couldn't be accessed," she continued, not looking at him.

"Yes."

A quavering smile curved her lips. She looked at him, her eyes cool, composed. It was a far cry from the way she was feeling inside. Her heart was shattering into a million pieces.

"Who else has seen the video?" she forced herself to ask.

"No one—not even I have," he confessed.

Her eyebrow lifted and she pursed her lips. A confession without even having to see the evidence. He was smooth, very smooth.

"I have to go," she suddenly said, placing her coffee cup on the table next to the memory stick.

"Where?" he demanded.

Her eyes glittered with tears before she blinked them away. Harlem had taught her too well for that.

But obviously not well enough, she thought, glancing at the flash drive one more time before she stepped away.

She didn't rush down the hallway to their bedroom. Behind her, she could hear Tarek's determined steps.

She needed space—time to breathe, to think. Telling Tarek the truth went against everything Harlem had taught her. Despite all the women that Harlem claimed to love, Idella believed there was only one that he truly did. His love nearly killed the woman, and Harlem had severed the relationship. It was the only time in Idella's life that she had witnessed Harlem Jones cry.

Her suitcase had been delivered shortly after her arrival, and she pulled it out of the closet now, placing it on the bed. Tarek watched her in silence as she began to fill it. His face was tight with emotion.

On her second pass, she couldn't stand the silence any longer. "I was nine when my mother died of a cocaine overdose," she said. "It was three in the morning, on July 14th. She took her last breath in a back alley, close to the building that would one day become my nightclub. It was miserably hot, even at that time of the morning. I was sleeping in the cardboard box we called home. I heard the death rattle of her last breath. That is what woke me, the strange rattling noise. I'll never forget the sound of it. I sat by her side, begging her not to leave me alone, crying out for help."

Idella didn't pause in her packing. Every item was folded with military precision. In a tone devoid of emotion, she continued.

"The thing about the streets is that you live and die there, alone. Help only comes to those who help themselves. The delivery truck drivers, early merchants, and other homeless people went about their business as if they couldn't hear me. They all ignored me... except for one," she said, pausing and staring into space for a moment before she moved back to gather more clothes.

"Who came?" he asked.

"Harlem Jones. A man larger than fiction—bigger than life." Her lips curved into a ghost of a smile.

She began folding her clothes again. She sensed Tarek's warm body before she felt his hands. A shiver of need ran through her when he slid his hands down her arms to her hands. She dropped the top she had been folding and stared blindly at their linked fingers.

"Tell me," he demanded in a low voice.

His breath caressed her cheek. She blinked rapidly to dispel the tears threatening to overflow. She had never been so emotional before.

"He came out of the darkness, took one look at me, and scooped me up into his arms. I remember everything so clearly. He told me not to cry because crying would be wasted on that woman. He said she never cared for the precious gem entrusted to her, and he took me to his townhouse. I had never been in a building so beautiful. The floors gleamed as if they were polished every day. I could see my reflection in them—a scrawny, scared little girl with eyes too big for her face. I soon discovered Harlem collected fine art and lost children. He was our Peter Pan and we were his Lost Boys."

"Who was Captain Hook?" he asked.

"Anyone and everyone." She breathed deeply. "I wasn't the first child that Harlem trained, but I believe I was the first one he fell in love with… thought of as his daughter. I always loved to sing. It soothed my mother… and me." She smiled at the memory. "It soothed Harlem as well. He had a grand piano and I had a natural talent for playing it by ear. Soon I was creating my music and singing."

"And…?" Tarek asked darkly. "You said he trained you, but I feel like it was for more than singing."

He caressed her soothingly. Idella relaxed back against him, closing her eyes and breathing in the delicious, evocative scent of him.

"He was an assassin—mostly for different governments, but he did some mercenary work as well." From Tarek's inhaled breath and the stiffening of his body, she could tell this was not what he was expecting. "He had a very high code of ethics. He was picky about the jobs he accepted… mostly. By the time I was twelve, Harlem had already used me on eleven missions."

Tarek's curse was loud in the otherwise quiet room.

Idella sighed. This would be difficult, but she needed him to understand how dangerous she was. "It was easy for me to slip in and out undetected. I was a quick study and an avid student. I killed my first man at fourteen. He was a trafficker: children, drugs, and money. His last illicit act was putting a hit on a congressional representative. That's why Harlem targeted him," she said.

She turned in his arms, wanting to see his eyes—wanting him to see hers. If they were doing this, she would not do it halfway and then wonder when the other shoe would drop. He had to understand that she wasn't who he thought she was.

"I could kill you in less than thirty seconds if I wanted, disappear, and no one would be the wiser," she said.

He groaned with desire and captured her lips in a deep, passionate kiss that stole her breath away.

She wasn't expecting *that* reaction at all, but her arms quickly wound around his neck and the familiar heat between her legs flared with a ravenousness need. When he finally lifted his head, she stared up at him with dazed eyes.

"It would be a glorious thirty seconds," he murmured.

Her lips twitched at his teasing remark. "This is the part where you are supposed to be horrified and run screaming for your bodyguards," she whispered against his lips.

"But you would spend all your time and energy killing them and would have none left for me," he protested.

She shook her head. "It would be a warm-up," she teased.

He leaned forward, bending her back over the bed. Her eyes widened when he shoved the suitcase out of their way, dumping it and the contents on the floor as they tumbled onto the bed. She hadn't known what to expect, but ripping each other's clothes off while they bit, sucked, kissed, and fought for supremacy had not been it!

She won the first battle, drawing hoarse cries from Tarek—but Tarek won the next. When he held her hands above her head, stretching her body out under him and plunging into her with deep, controlled strokes, she begged him for more.

Lying in the aftermath of their lovemaking, Idella ran her fingers through his coarse chest hair. She loved the way it felt under her fingers. She was so deeply in love with Tarek, she was ruined.

Loving someone interferes with your thinking. You start to make stupid mistakes—mistakes that will get you and the person you love killed.

Harlem had warned them countless times.

"What are you thinking?" he asked.

"Hmm...." She laughed. "Now that you know who I am, how am I ever going to kill you?"

Twelve

Tarek eyed Idella with an amused expression as she huffed and rolled her eyes at him. She tapped her fingernail on the arm of the chair and pursed her lips. He sat behind his desk, she was settled in her own seat beside him, and they waited for the meeting she had reluctantly agreed to.

When Adel, Dhamar, and Emin entered his office, Idella immediately became relaxed, the glamorous singer persona washing over her—until Butrus entered a moment later. Her eyes slightly narrowed and she surreptitiously palmed the decorative letter opener lying near the corner of his desk. He would have missed it if he hadn't been watching her so closely.

"Idella," each of the men greeted—except for Butrus.

It was like watching two equally matched predators sizing each other up. Tarek didn't try to hide how entertaining it was, and with a sudden scowl, Idella crumpled a blank piece of paper and tossed it at his face. He laughed in surprise.

"You don't have to be enjoying yourself so much," she growled.

"I can't help it. Even your threats to kill me are enjoyable." He grinned.

Idella and Butrus's eyes locked, her head tilting with a silent warning, but he moved in sudden attack and she responded by catching the heavy seat of her chair with her foot and tossing it at Adel, Emin, and Dhamar as she rolled over Butrus's back and came up holding his left arm behind his back and the letter opener against his neck.

Her eyes were cold, her lips pressed in a straight line. Tarek had seen no one more dangerous or more beautiful in his life. She was a wolf in sheep's clothing, and it felt like every drop of blood in his body had gone straight to his cock.

"*Habibi,* please don't kill Butrus," he gently requested.

Idella didn't move. The letter opener had barely pierced Butrus's skin. Her eyes were focused on the other three men in the room, but Tarek could sense that she was acutely aware of every move he made.

"Pay up, *ragazzi,*" Dhamar said with a grin, holding out his hand and wiggling his fingers.

"Half—" Butrus growled, wincing when the tip of the sharp letter opener pricked his throat more deeply when he spoke. "—of that is mine, Dhamar."

Adel and Emin pulled their wallets out, extracted some cash, and slapped it in Dhamar's open palm. Idella carefully released Butrus and stepped away. The letter opener disappeared.

Tarek imagined slowly taking off her clothes to find it. He might do that later if the letter opener didn't reappear on his desk—or maybe he would bend her over his desk even if she did return it.

Dhamar counted out half of the money and offered it to Butrus. Idella sent a cold glare in Tarek's direction. Surprised, he shook his head at her unspoken accusation.

"I didn't say anything," he promised.

Idella moved to lean against the wall close to the door. Butrus touched his throat while Emin righted the heavy chair with an impressed expression. Tarek motioned for the men to be seated in various chairs around the room as he brought Idella's chair back to its rightful place next to his.

Idella didn't move however, the chair beside Tarek's remaining empty, so Tarek didn't sit either. The two of them faced off from opposite sides of the room, he behind his desk, she by the door. Emin, Dhamar, Adel, and Butrus all adjusted their chairs to have a better view of Idella.

"It *was* you at the Business building," Butrus said just before Adel stated with conviction, "I can name on two fingers the number of people who could have taken the shot you did and I'm one of them."

Dhamar and Emin looked at each other and shrugged.

"We are still eating crow because you slipped past us," Emin said.

Tarek noticed a slight relaxation in Idella's shoulders. He walked over to her and tenderly stroked her hand, giving her time to realize that she was in no danger from any of the men in this room.

She finally tore her watchful eyes away from his team to look at him. Tarek gently caressed her cheek. She lowered her eyelashes, concealing her thoughts, and he found he didn't like that.

"I'm sorry. I had no idea they would do that," he murmured.

"It was foolish of them. I could have killed them," she replied.

He cupped her cheek and tilted her head back so she was forced to look at him. In her eyes he saw worry, regret—and a desire to flee.

"They would have deserved it," he stated.

A few seconds passed in frozen silence before her lips curved in the tiniest of smiles. He leaned forward and kissed her. He didn't release her lips until she responded.

"We need your help," he said. "Coldhouse is still alive."

She hesitated, glancing at the four men who were trying to act like they weren't watching them. Butrus fussed with his blood-stained handkerchief and the others looked at various points around the room.

"I'm leaving to go after him," she confessed.

Tarek shook his head. "Not alone, *habibi*. You will never be alone again."

Tarek lifted her hand to his lips and kissed her knuckles. She opened her mouth to respond but instead her shoulders stiffened and her expression went blank.

"There are *three* people who could have made the shot, Adel. You, myself, and one other," she said.

Adel narrowed his eyes. "Who is the third?"

Idella just smiled that secretive, sexy Sphinx smile she had and didn't respond.

"What leads do you have?" she asked, sinking onto the chair she had vacated a few minutes before as if nothing unusual had just happened.

Butrus exchanged a glance with Tarek before he gave his report. "An angler reported seeing an injured man leaving a pleasure craft that had been reported stolen. The local authorities are investigating."

"I'd like Dhamar and Butrus to check out the boat and interview the owner," Tarek said.

"I'll check security footage in the area," Adel said.

Emin opened his mouth before he shrugged. "I was going to offer my protection to Idella, but I think I'll just keep an eye on Tarek and have her watch my back," he said with an easy grin.

"I have my own sources I can check," she said.

Tarek wanted to protest her involvement in this, but he knew deep down that trying to stop her was the best way to drive her away.

"Keep me posted," Tarek said.

The men rose to their feet. Tarek waited until they had all left his office and closed the door before he gently pulled Idella to her feet. Her eyes locked with his and he saw a reserve in them he hadn't seen before.

"Idella, *habibi*," he murmured, caressing her cheek.

She gave him a smile that didn't reach her eyes. A chill stabbed at his heart.

"I need to… go," she said, hesitating on the last word as if it pained her to say it.

He threaded his fingers through her hair. She tried to move away from him and his grip tightened. The distant expression in her eyes flickered and he saw an unbearable anguish for a split second. He whispered a curse, dragged her into his arms, and captured her lips.

She didn't respond… at first. When her lips finally parted, they kissed with a mad passion. He boosted her onto the desk. She grabbed a fistful of his shirt as she leaned back, bringing him with her. He held her in an iron grip as his tongue stroked hers.

"Tarek," Idella said, half moan half protest, changing her grip to a flat palm pushing slightly against his shoulder.

He pulled back an inch. "We will go after Coldhouse together, *habibi*. You never have to do this alone again," he vowed, tangling his hands in her hair and resting his forehead against hers.

Idella shook her head, the movement tiny against his grip on her hair. Her beautiful hazel eyes shimmered with tears before she closed them with a shudder and sighed into his mouth.

"I'm not sure this is a good idea. I seem to lose all common sense when I'm around you," she confessed.

"Not all. You know that you should trust me," he said.

Idella's soft breath caressed his lips and she trailed her fingers along his cheek. He held onto her when she tried to pull away again, and she kissed him before she gently pushed against his chest. He let her go.

"There are advantages to me going after Coldhouse alone," she said as she straightened and left him to stand by the window.

"What advantages?"

"This mission has dragged on for a very long time. My superiors are impatient—so am I—but if I do not complete my mission soon, assets will be sent to eliminate my distractions." She paused and turned to face him. "I will terminate anyone who tries to kill you. I will terminate anyone who *gives the order* to kill you. All hell will break loose."

"Your partner, this is why he was upset that you saved my life, isn't it? You never told me who he was," Tarek said.

"He won't harm you. But yes... that is one of the reasons he was upset. Bronislav and the Coldhouse brothers need to die. I'm not supposed to care about the collateral damage, but you know that I do. I would set my old world on fire for you. It would be better if I don't have to."

Thirteen

Border of Jawahir and Simdan:

Anderson Coldhouse collapsed on the ground, gritting his teeth to keep from moaning out loud. He clutched his injured arm, cursing under his breath as he scooted back against a rock. Leaning his head back, he slowly counted until the pain in his arm and leg turned to a dull, constant thud.

Burns, cuts, and bruises littered his body. What the fight and the explosion from the speedboat hadn't caused, his trek across the desert had. He had lost his communication equipment in the wreckage. It had been too dangerous to go back to the safe house. The streets had been crawling with the Jawahir Royal Military.

He shakily took a swig of water from the oil-sealed bag he had taken from the farmer a day ago. Spilling a little of the precious liquid on his shirt, he leaned his head back and stared out across the sand and dirt landscape. If they hadn't been found, there should be some much-needed supplies in a cave less than a mile from where he was now. If there was one thing he had learned over the years, it was to have a back-up plan that no one else knew about—including his brother.

He gritted his teeth as he pulled back the torn material covering his leg and studied the eight-inch gash nearly a half-inch deep in his thigh. The wound was swollen and angry.

His cotton pants chafed against the burned skin on his calf. His shoulder had been dislocated, and while he had popped it back into place, it was gruelingly painful whenever he jarred it.

He had multiple burns and cuts. The burns were the worst since they were aggravated by the heat of the desert.

"Fuck!" he hissed, leaning back and lifting the pouch to his lips again.

He drained the last of his precious water and closed his eyes. In another mile, he should have time to rest, deal with his wounds, and plan his revenge. He would be over the border, out of Jawahir and into the safety of Simdan where Zulfirquar Kaffir ruled with a tyrannical fist. The man was on Bronislav's pay list and had given support to Colin.

Anderson gave a heartfelt sigh as he thought about how the bitch from New York had not only survived all his attempts to kill her over the last few years, but when he contacted her this time, she had tattled to several people. And then the Crown Prince of Jawahir himself came to her rescue! Anderson growled his frustration.

The man had not fought like a privileged monarch and he had held up under the beating Anderson gave him a month ago. His moves on the boat had been as skilled as any of the men that Colin employed.

"I'll kill them all if it is the last thing I do," he vowed hoarsely.

He braced his hand against the rock behind him and pushed himself up, hissing with pain when he put weight on his leg. He stumbled, almost falling, but caught himself at the last second. Gritting his teeth, he breathed through his nose and looked out over the landscape.

Vengeance will be mine, and this time I won't fail, he silently swore.

"I don't like it. It could be a trap," Tarek growled from the doorway.

Idella was packing again. This time it was because her persona as an international singer was needed. When she was first offered a gig headlining in Dima, the Simdan capital, for Sheikh Zulfirquar Kaffir's special event, all she felt was revulsion. She knew more about Kaffir than he realized, including the connection between the tyrannical warlord and his foreign supporters—which was exactly why she was going. Her band and crew would meet her there. She was dreading telling Raja about it.

"Of course it's a trap," she replied.

Tarek's heated curses sent a shiver down Idella's spine. She didn't know if it was the idea of him being upset or the amount of passion in the words, but it definitely drew a physical response from her. Just before he wrapped his arms around her, she turned and sent him sprawling on the bed, caging him between her thighs.

They kissed passionately. With a quick movement, she suddenly found herself beneath his taut body. She ran her nails through his hair. He grabbed her wrists and pinned them above her head with one hand. She gasped, rolling her hips under him.

"You know I love it when you…." She noticed his eyes blazing down at her with a combination of anger, fear, and desire, and she trailed off. The only sound was their heavy breaths. His gaze slid down to the gap in her shirt and her nipples pebbled and ached. She lightly tested the strength of his hold, and heat rushed through her when he kept her immobile.

"This isn't a game, Idella. Kaffir is crazy. He murdered his brother and his brother's family, including the women and children."

"I can handle it, Tarek. I was made for this."

Tarek groaned, nuzzling her cheek for a moment. "We both know that Anderson Coldhouse is there. What we don't know is where Colin is."

"A compound in Lithuania. Bronislav is in his mansion outside of Moscow. The one *you* need to worry about is Rashid al Hamid. He never left Jawahir."

Tarek's fingers tightened on her wrists and he shook his head. "How you know all of this is scary."

She laughed and his eyes immediately moved back to her breasts. Idella bit her lip, feeling hot all over again. If she didn't get out of here, she was going to miss her flight. He cupped her breast, thumbing her nipple.

"I need to leave," she whispered on a moan of need. She arched into his hand and trembled.

He leaned forward, holding her gaze. "I'm coming with you," he announced before kissing her breathless again.

Tarek kept his eyes locked on Idella's face as she sat across from him on the private jet flying them to Dima. She was on her laptop, her fingers moving rapidly and forcefully over the keyboard. Whoever she was chatting with must not like what she was telling them. It was strange because anyone else would probably not have noticed the subtle flash of emotion in her eyes or the slight tightening of her lips.

He noticed everything about her, from the exotic fragrance she used to the way her quick mind captured and categorized every detail around her. He fought the urge to caress the slight crease between her eyes.

"Is something wrong?" he asked.

She looked up and gave him a crooked smile. "Nothing I can't handle," she replied.

His focus sharpened and she sighed.

"My... friend is not happy that I am going into Simdan. Like you, he thinks it is a trap and too dangerous."

"… Is he the man who was with you when you found me?"

"Yes." Her eyes softened with emotion.

Jealousy flared through him. He reminded himself that Idella had been a virgin.

"Who is he to you?" he asked, his voice a touch sharper than he meant.

Amusement made her eyes twinkle. She stretched out her long leg and placed her bare foot between his legs, teasing his groin with her toes. He cupped her foot, gently massaging her instep. Her lips parted on a tiny gasp and she blushed as she looked away. He catalogued that little tidbit away for later analysis.

She bit her lip, looking down at her laptop before she closed the lid and set it on the seat next to her. Apprehension was in her eyes as she surveyed the interior of the plane. The steward was in the front with his bodyguards.

"What I tell you goes no further than between you and me, Tarek. The information I share affects far more than myself," she quietly said.

"You can trust me, Idella," he promised. He desperately wanted to be one of the few people that Idella trusted. It was a trust he would never betray.

She bowed her head, took a deep breath, and stared at him, her lips curving in a rueful smile. The smile contained sadness, but also serenity and resolve.

"You know him by his code name Hamlet. His real name is Raja Hadi," she said.

Tarek's eyes widened, immediately making the connection. Hadi was not a common name, and he had just warned Idella about the fate of Simdan's royal family. King Suhail Hadi, Queen Farrah, and their three children, Raja, Fariha, and Nagi had been murdered by the Queen's uncle, Zulfirquar Kaffir. Only the bodies of the King and Queen were recovered. It was believed the children were disposed of discreetly to reduce international condemnation.

"He survived?" Tarek hissed.

Idella nodded. "Harlem found him and brought him home. Raja became a big brother to me. We often work together."

Tarek was silent as he digested the information. A sheikh of Simdan, alive— If Raja were to return, it would change the dynamics of the entire region!

He looked up at Idella. She nodded.

"When will he arrive?"

She leaned her head back and sighed. "I told him not to come. We need to keep track of Colin... but, yes, I would be shocked if he doesn't come. He wants Kaffir dead, but he won't do anything to jeopardize the mission or endanger me."

"That's what you were just arguing with him about?"

"That... and I told him you were with me... and that you—and your personal bodyguards—know about me."

"What did he say?"

Her lips formed a wry smile. "Let's just say he is not any more pleased with that revelation than he is with me performing for Kaffir."

"What are your plans? What do you think Kaffir wants?"

She lifted a slender shoulder. "I plan to find Anderson Coldhouse and kill him, of course. As for why Kaffir is paying over a million dollars for a private performance, I'll find out when I get there. The only thing that really bothers me is that my band and crew will be there. They... aren't aware of my side job."

"Perhaps I should have asked what can I do?"

Her eyes softened. "Let's assess the situation when we get there. The two biggest things are: don't get between me and my targets and don't get yourself killed," she quietly replied.

He caressed the inside of her calf, loving how his touch made her eyelids droop and her lips part. She was breathtakingly beautiful. Everything inside him wanted to wrap her up and lock her away. He couldn't stand the thought of anyone hurting her. The idea of her being near some of the most dangerous men in the world curdled his stomach.

He glanced over her shoulder to the back of the plane and made eye contact with Dhamar and Butrus. A man had to do what a man had to do to keep his woman safe.

Fourteen

"Wow! Would you get a load of this place? Why did Wallace book us here again?" Chia asked, looking around the room with wide, wary eyes.

"Maybe he wanted to offend your prudish sense of outrage," Calvin teased.

"You obviously haven't seen Chia's bedroom," Tyler joked.

"Neither have you, Ty," she retorted.

"I can dream," Ty said with a cheeky grin.

Idella was having difficulty taking her eyes off the room herself. She wiggled her nose with distaste. It looked like something out of a prurient nightmare. She took in the gaudy red satin drapes everywhere and the lewd statues with distaste.

"Someone has some really weird fantasies," Midnight muttered.

Idella blinked at the woman standing next to her. She was seldom surprised, but Midnight's appearance as part of the crew was shocking. Midnight studied the ceiling with disgust and Idella looked up as well. Murals of nude men and women having aberrant orgies were painted onto several panels which were outlined by garish gold molding across the expansive room.

"What are you doing here?" she asked.

Midnight shrugged. "Bugs said you needed security and Wallace offered a shitload of money."

Idella gritted her teeth. *Bugs* should have told no one about this assignment! Damn-it-all-to-hell, she would definitely need to have a talk with her mysteriously protective friend.

"Have you met Bugs before?" Idella asked, suddenly curious.

Midnight raised an eyebrow at her and moved off to explore the room without answering. Idella's gaze lingered on the scarf covering the lower half of Midnight's face for a moment as she listened to Chia mutter, "Idella, I swear if those dirty old men masturbate while you sing, I'm going to shove—okay, forget that thought. They might *enjoy* having a drum stick shoved up where the sun don't shine. I'm just saying, if it gets kinky, I'm outta here!"

Idella grinned with amusement. "I'll be sure to insist that everyone stays fully clothed during the performance."

A group of men in various shapes, sizes, and clothing styles entered the ballroom, and Idella turned to face them. A short man spearheaded the group, his bodyguards flared behind him like a looming shadow. Idella's group fanned out to get a better view of the meeting, all of them except for Midnight.

"You are indeed as beautiful as your pictures," Sheikh Zulfirquar Kaffir greeted.

Idella had been about to ignore Kaffir's outstretched hands but there was no need when Midnight stepped in between them. The woman was holding a microphone and long cable coiled in her hands, and her body language conveyed superiority. Idella fought back a grin when Kaffir stopped short and scowled, his hands falling to his sides without ever touching Idella.

"Security," Midnight introduced. "And you are?"

Two men behind Kaffir stepped forward. Midnight never took her eyes off of Kaffir, who was glaring at her, his mouth twisted with contempt.

"It's alright, Midnight. I have this," Idella quietly stated behind her.

Midnight tilted her head to the side, as if assessing Kaffir and finding him… lacking. When she walked away, she knocked into one of Kaffir's bodyguards. The man growled an insult which Midnight laughed at.

Subtle, Midnight. Real subtle, Idella thought with a sigh.

Idella turned her attention to Kaffir. She gave the man one of her famous smiles, hoping to ease the tension. It was hard to keep a straight face when Midnight and the other band members rolled their eyes behind Kaffir's back.

"Sheikh Kaffir, thank you for your invitation. My manager, Wallace, didn't give me many details about your special event. Perhaps you can share more about your expectations before tomorrow night's performance."

A lascivious smile curved Kaffir's wide mouth. "I would be happy to discuss the event. Perhaps at dinner tonight?"

"We look forward to joining you," Tarek interjected in a deep, smooth voice.

Idella kept her smile in place while Tarek stepped around the group of six men and slid his arm around her waist. She tilted her head towards him, her expression conveying affection, as if she *wasn't* imagining stuffing him in a closet so she could work this mission alone. Kaffir's eyes narrowed and he sneered. When he noticed Tarek's cane, however, hints of satisfaction appeared in his expression.

"Prince Tarek, I was informed that you had arrived with Idella. I must say that I was… surprised."

Tarek pulled her closer and Idella resisted the urge to pinch him. Between Midnight and Tarek, getting any information out of Kaffir was going to be like having her wisdom teeth extracted without anesthesia—all four of them at the same time. All she needed now was for Raja to appear.

She pulled out of Tarek's grasp and threaded her arm through Kaffir's with a charming smile. "Zulfirquar, why don't you give me a tour of the palace? I've never been in a palace before."

She gave a pointed look at Tarek. The flash of sardonic anger in his eyes and the tightening around his mouth warned her that she would pay for that little jab about never being in a palace later, but if she had to deal with cozying up to Kaffir for the sake of the mission, Tarek could certainly deal with her being catty and pretending there was a wedge between them.

"With pleasure," Kaffir wheezed, caressing her hand.

"Tarek, would you be a love and brief Midnight on your security? I'd hate for her to get in an altercation with any of them by mistake."

Tarek tilted his head in a brief nod. "With pleasure, *habibi*," he mockingly replied.

She shot Tarek a grateful smile and steered Kaffir toward the exit. She knew that while Tarek wasn't pleased about her maneuver, he understood what she was doing and that she would update him later when they were alone. Once they were in the corridor, she paused, giving Kaffir the lead.

Kaffir turned to the right and guided her along a long polished corridor. Idella listened as he pointed out various great works of art. She murmured the appropriate responses while mentally documenting every detail. After several minutes, the group of men surrounding them began to peel away until it was just her and two of Kaffir's bodyguards who walked several feet behind them.

"The artwork is lovely, but I would really love for you to tell me about the palace and your lovely country. I've always had a love for history," Idella invited.

"You have never been to Simdan before?" Kaffir asked with a raised eyebrow.

She laughed and waved her free hand. "It is a little difficult for me to get in and out without being seen by the media. Dima appears to be a lovely city, though I've only seen it from the plane as we were landing. If I had known about your invitation sooner, I would have done more research. I'm embarrassed by my lack of knowledge."

"The history is not as important as the present and the future."

Kaffir brought her hand toward his lips. She suppressed a shiver of distaste. Instead, she gave him a smile as she pulled her hand free before he could press his lips to her skin. She walked away, adding just a touch more sway to her hips to keep the insult from stinging—and making Kaffir want more.

Like that will ever happen.

"Why is Tarek Saif-Ad-Din here?" Kaffir suddenly demanded.

Idella looked over her shoulder at Kaffir with a surprised expression. "He had a plane and was willing to fly me here on short notice."

Kaffir walked closer. The maneuver was done to intimidate her. She debated whether she should act like he wanted her to and decided to pretend she was unaware of the danger. She returned her focus to the intricately carved support beams.

"The structure of the palace is beautiful. It must be hundreds of years old," she marveled.

"Are you lovers?" Kaffir demanded.

She wanted to tell him it was none of his fucking business. She wished she could kill the bastard right then and there. Instead, Idella looked at Kaffir again and blinked as if stunned that he would dare to ask her something so personal.

"I came here because you offered a lot of money to hear me perform. My personal life is none of your concern, Sheikh Kaffir. I hope you understand that I prefer to keep the two separate," she calmly replied.

Kaffir's thick lips curled. "It matters not," he replied.

"Good. I would hate to have to cancel my performance."

The sound of a door opening farther down the hallway drew her attention. A man at the far end stood in the shadows. She could feel his eyes on her before he disappeared through another door. There was a slight limp in his gait. Her stomach knotted. While she didn't get a clear view of his face, she would bet her favorite sniper rifle that Anderson Coldhouse was in the palace.

"Let us continue your tour," Kaffir said, holding out his arm again.

Anderson watched the screen as Kaffir escorted Idella around the lower section of the palace. He couldn't believe his good fortune when she arrived with Tarek Saif-Ad-Din. The second screen showed Tarek and his guards walking through the room where tomorrow night's performance was to be held. Tarek was talking to a woman from Idella's band.

As much as he would love to kill the five men, he wouldn't… yet. No, his plans involved taking his sweet time with Tarek and his exquisite mistress. The only hitch was Kaffir. The man did not want an international incident on his turf. Anderson would need to entice them away from Simdan.

He mimicked pulling the trigger on a gun and pointed it at Tarek with a malicious grin. Kaffir had delivered his prize as promised. Now, for them both to enjoy the fruits of it.

Fifteen

"I saw Anderson Coldhouse," Idella said, removing her earrings as she slowly walked around the bedroom suite they had been given. This was the first chance they'd had alone.

Tarek stiffened and looked sharply at her. "Idella...," he cautioned. He glanced around the room. Butrus and Emin had searched it for listening devices and video earlier, but he still didn't trust that the room wasn't bugged.

She pulled a small device out of her pocket and placed it on the night-stand. "No video, and any sound will be useless," she promised.

Tarek shook his head in wonder and cynicism, and slid his arms around her waist. "Do you always carry such equipment?"

A sultry laugh slipped from her. "The paparazzi are far worse than any spy group. I've found all kinds of hidden microphones and video cameras in my dressing rooms over the years. I've been careful for so many years, I couldn't believe that I forgot about it when I was staying at the apartment with you."

He tightened his hold briefly, and she covered his hand with her own.

"You've never had a normal life," he reflected with remorse.

"And you think being a prince is normal?" she teased.

He ran his lips along the smooth column of her neck.

"Mm, you have no idea how good that feels," she breathed.

Oh, he did know how good it felt, but he couldn't allow himself to be distracted for long. "Where did you see Coldhouse?"

"Second level, going into a room at the far end of the south corridor. I'll do some reconnaissance after dinner to find him again."

"I need to let Butrus and the others know."

She nodded. "Tell them not to chase him. I need them to protect my band and crew. Chia, Calvin, and Tyler have no clue what is going on."

Tarek frowned. "What about the other woman, Midnight?"

She turned in his arms. "Midnight is… different. She can take care of herself and is already exploring. She hates being cooped up, especially at night. As for us, we should be getting ready for the dinner Kaffir invited us to."

He didn't move. "Combine Coldhouse with Kaffir and this situation is less than ideal," Tarek groused.

Idella gently caressed his side where he had been wounded. "No situation where you are in danger is ideal for me," she said.

There were too many variables that could go wrong, and it didn't help that he wasn't a hundred percent yet. His thoughts grew darker as he changed his clothes.

Tarek did not enjoy playing these games with the people he loved at stake, but he would do whatever it took. Idella had suggested that he act like his leg still pained him to throw Kaffir off. She had also suggested that Butrus and the others take his private jet back. In the end, they had compromised with Dhamar and Emin coming to the palace with him and Adel and Butrus remaining with the jet to ensure that it was not compromised should they need to leave in a hurry.

He adjusted his tie, his expression softening when Idella soothed a strand of his hair back from his forehead before kissing him. She looked stunning as usual in silver heels and a cream-colored evening gown that accented her slender figure, yet covered it modestly. His eyes widened and he swallowed when she set her foot on a low table to adjust the sheath strapped to her thigh and he noticed that she was wearing stockings with a garter belt. He was looking forward to peeling them off her later. The amused expression on her face told him she was reading his mind.

"Let's get this over with," he growled.

Idella touched the intricate ear cuff she was wearing. The platinum piece was a pave design with tiny diamonds, sexy as hell, and disguised the fact that she was wearing an ear piece. Midnight had given her the 'special delivery' as they were about to enter the dining room. It wasn't hard to guess who had given it to Midnight. Raja had returned to Simdan and was somewhere in the palace.

Chia, Calvin, and Tyler were huddled together as far away from Kaffir and his generals as they could get. Ty shot her a relieved expression when she entered the room. Kaffir's eyes swept over her with anticipatory greed and calculating appraisal.

She covered her revulsion with a charming smile. There were times that Harlem's insistence that she learn to bury her true feelings was useful, and this was one of them.

"Gentlemen," she greeted.

"You are truly a diamond in the desert, Idella," Kaffir responded. "May I introduce three of my most decorated generals: General Amit, General Hatim, and General Gamar."

"It's a pleasure to meet you," Idella replied with a bow of her head to each unsmiling man. She wound her arm through Tarek's and smiled up at him. "I believe you already know Prince Tarek Saif-Ad-Din."

"We've met," Tarek responded.

"Shall we be seated?" Kaffir offered.

"Absolutely. I'm famished," she replied.

Idella didn't miss the looks that passed between the three generals. Her senses were tingling. Ty's forced laugh drew her attention to her band members. Having them there was like placing mice in a tank of hungry vipers.

She sank into the chair to the right of Kaffir. General Amit sat next to her while Tarek was ushered to the left of Kaffir across the table. General Gamar sat next to him, and the band sat further down the table.

"How are you healing, Tarek?" Kaffir asked.

Idella picked up her wine glass and sipped it.

"I'm nearly back to my old self," Tarek answered.

"Did you find out who was behind the attack?" General Amit asked.

Idella listened as Tarek easily dodged the loaded questions. She smiled and made appropriate comments when necessary. Kaffir looked toward the end of the table with a frown.

"Where is the other woman? The one who covers her face?"

"Midnight? She's a loner. She doesn't do people," Chia said.

"She doesn't do daylight either. I think she's a vampire," Calvin added with a laugh.

"Midnight is uncomfortable in social settings," Idella explained.

Kaffir's eyes narrowed. "Why does she cover her face?"

Idella lifted her chin. "Midnight's reasons are her own. I do not judge. This isn't a matter of concern, is it? After all, many of the women in this region prefer to conceal their features."

"It is of no concern, just curiosity. I am happy that you do not conceal your lovely face," he replied.

"Be careful, Zulfirquar, or I might think you are trying to turn my head," Idella teased. Her comm immediately sounded with Raja's snarling voice and Midnight's disgust.

"What the hell are you playing at?!"

"That is so gross!"

Idella was amazed she didn't flinch. She was also impressed that Tarek didn't come unglued, though from the piercing glint in his eyes, he was keeping a running tally of all the things he'd like to punish her for —in the most pleasant of ways, of course. She was briefly distracted by very sexy thoughts of what that punishment might entail before she brought her dirty mind back to the mission.

This is why it is better to work alone sometimes, she thought.

She lifted her wine glass and took another sip as she scanned the room. A lone figure standing off to the side caught her attention. He was dressed as a waiter. Their eyes briefly connected before he stepped back into the shadows and disappeared. Her fingers tightened on the stem of the crystal wineglass and she lowered her eyes—Raja was even closer than she realized.

As they finished their meal, Kaffir said, "I hope you don't mind if I kidnap Tarek from you. I would like to discuss some state business with him in private."

She bowed her head slightly. "Of course not. It is always better for me to get a good night's rest before a performance. They can be quite exhausting. Tomorrow will be busy with rehearsals and final set up."

From his seat beside her, Kaffir leaned far too close to her, grasped her hand, and brought it to his mouth. He lingered there, pressing his lips to her skin. She raised an eyebrow at him.

Tarek pushed his chair back and rose to his feet. Kaffir's fingers tightened around her hand, preventing her from pulling it out of his grip without making a scene. On Idella's other side, Amit stood up. Gamar and Hatim did too, looming next to Tarek. Her band members froze, their unease rising as they watched the scene unfold.

Kaffir and Tarek faced each other across the table, Kaffir not bothering to stand. Tarek's grip on his cane tightened, eyes promising murder.

Idella surged to her feet, tugging her hand free. "Thank you for a lovely dinner. I believe I'll walk back with Chia, Calvin, and Ty. I have a few last minute changes to tomorrow's performance program that I would like to discuss with them. Gentlemen."

She walked around the table, stopped in front of Tarek, and slid her hand up his arm. He tore his eyes away from Kaffir to look at her, gently grasped her chin, and kissed her. Her breath caught in her throat. The kiss was rough, passionate, and lasted long enough that there was no doubt that she belonged to him.

"I won't be long, *raqisat alqamar*. Emin will go with you," he murmured.

Her lips tingling from his branding, she bowed her head and smiled her goodbyes to Kaffir and his generals. Chia was staring at her with a *WTF* expression while Calvin and Tyler fought to hide their grins. The guys made it almost to the door before Ty spoke.

"Well, we know who the alpha in the room is," Ty muttered.

"Yes," she quietly agreed, trying not to laugh. "Yes, we do."

Sixteen

"You shouldn't be playing games with my uncle," Raja growled.

"You shouldn't be in the country, much less the palace, with the man who would get off while killing you," she retorted as she grabbed a pair of black cargo trousers and a matching long-sleeved shirt.

A snort from the corner drew her attention. She scowled when she noticed the movement of a foot in the shadows.

"What is it about everyone congregating in my room? Aren't you supposed to be protecting my band?"

Raja matched her scowl when he realized that Midnight was in the room with them. The way she could blend in with the dark was seriously spooky.

"I found Coldhouse. There was no way to kill him without raising a shitstorm. Plus, I figured you might want to do the honors. By the way, the guy has some serious issues—he was muttering to himself as he watched you have dinner from the basement or dungeon or whatever you call it. This place is seriously depressing," Midnight replied.

"It wasn't always this way," Raja muttered.

Sympathy swept through Idella but so did fear. It burned like a bed of coals in her stomach.

"Emil and Dhamar?" she asked.

"Last I saw they were standing outside the room where Tarek, Grossman, and his minions are having a drink."

"Ok. Midnight, I'd like you to stay close to Chia and the guys. If you get any sense of danger, get them out of here."

"Sure thing," Midnight replied. "Bugs gave me a detailed diagram of the palace and I found some really interesting hidden passages while I was exploring earlier."

Midnight stood up, and the dim light of the bedside lamp washed over her. The younger woman looked more like an apparition than a real person. She was dressed all in black from her boots to the black cap she wore over her raven-colored hair. Her face was covered by a matching bandana. Only her eyes were visible and even those were outlined with a heavy black liner and smokey eyeshadow.

"Keep your mic on. I'll let you know if I find anything," Midnight said.

Idella watched as the woman walked over to a section of the wall and ran her fingers along a crevice. The faint sound of a click preceded the wall opening up to reveal a narrow passage.

Idella turned to Raja with alarm. "I need to know about these hidden passages. If Kaffir knows about them, he could slit our throats while we sleep."

Raja shook his head. "He doesn't know about them. Only my father and myself—and Midnight, who apparently has a knack for finding hidden passages—know about them. This is how I escaped the night Kaffir attacked my family. He never found out, I'm sure of it."

"I'll still place a monitor on it. I'm not going to trust that he or someone else hasn't discovered them. Can we get to Coldhouse through them?" she asked.

"Probably." He paused. "I'll warn you now, Idella, if I get close enough to my uncle, I will kill him. I know our superiors told us to leave my uncle alone for the moment, but this is personal."

She dipped her head in agreement. "I won't stand in your way."

Tarek relaxed in the high-back seat, holding a crystal glass of bourbon in one hand and casually caressing the handle of his cane with the other. Across from him, Kaffir sat with his own glass. They were alone except for Gamar. Out of the three generals, Gamar was the one that made Tarek the wariest—not that Amit or Hatim were any less lethal.

"Why did you invite Idella here?" he asked.

"How could I not? She is beautiful, sexy, and has a voice that wraps around a man and makes him dream of the many possibilities that could be enjoyed with her. Wouldn't you agree?"

Ire surged in Tarek, but he kept it hidden behind an icy façade. He knew Kaffir was trying to push him into an emotional reaction. He also knew something Kaffir didn't—that Idella could snap the miserable little toad's neck if she wanted.

"I agree she is all of those things. It still surprises me you would be interested in an American jazz singer. I would have thought you would be interested in more... traditional music," he remarked.

"I am a man who appreciates many sounds... especially coming from such a fascinating woman," Kaffir commented. "She has certainly entranced you. You have followed her here like an adoring pet. Or did you have another reason to come?"

Tarek lifted a shoulder. "She is exquisite, but yes, this was an opportunity to pay a diplomatic visit. You are aware that the attack on Qadir and myself occurred near the border with Simdan. The men responsible escaped into your country. I was hoping you might assist in their capture."

Kaffir's eyes narrowed. Gamar stepped closer and said, "The perpetrators were local tribesmen intending to rob you. They have been dealt with."

Tarek lifted an eyebrow. "I can assure you, General Gamar, those were not local tribesmen. You forget that I was there. I have the scars to prove it. No, these were foreigners, with sophisticated weaponry, specialized military vehicles, and other tactical equipment. They killed eight of my men in cold blood. Eight men who were highly trained."

"Our intelligence tells us that several of your attackers were killed in return, but not by you or your highly trained men. Someone else," Gamar responded.

Gamar was much better at hiding his emotions than Kaffir was. In fact, the man's eyes appeared devoid of any feelings at all, but it seemed Gamar had no idea that the sniper had been sitting a mere few feet from him during dinner.

"Unfortunately, I wasn't in any position to see who might have come to our aid," he lightly replied. "I was wounded and left for dead."

"And yet this person, that you claim you do not know, saved your life and later assisted in the rescue of your brother," Gamar reflected.

Tarek paused. After a moment, he decided to follow Gamar's lead. Sometimes it *was* better to reveal a little information in order to gain more.

"Anderson and Colin Coldhouse were behind the attacks. I know that Anderson is still in Simdan. I am asking for your support in apprehending him."

"Locating him might be difficult. Simdan is a large country with many places where a man could hide," Kaffir replied.

"Then I politely request that you look the other way while I do," he responded.

Kaffir swirled the liquid in his glass, a calculating expression on his face. "I might look away... possibly even assist you in finding Anderson Coldhouse."

"For a price?" Tarek guessed.

Kaffir chuckled. The sound came out between a wheeze and choked snarl. It reminded Tarek of fingernails on a chalkboard.

"More of an exchange... between friends, of course."

"And what would this *exchange* be?"

"The beautiful Idella's company for a short period of time in exchange for handing you Anderson Coldhouse."

Tarek set his crystal glass down on the end table with a forceful thunk and rose to his feet, tightly gripping the handle of his cane. It took every ounce of discipline in his body not to pull the sword secreted in the cane's shaft and impale Kaffir's puffy body with it.

"Idella is not for barter or for sale. I will not hesitate to kill any man who tries to harm her. Now, if you will excuse me, I believe it is time I retired for the evening."

Kaffir rose to his feet and coldly stared at him. Tarek ignored both men and exited the room. It was that or kill the sons-of-bitches.

A ball of rage roiled in his stomach as he walked through the corridors with Dhamar. Kaffir's guards followed them.

"It was a mistake to come here," he growled in frustration.

Dhamar's glance told him he agreed. When they reached the quarters assigned to Idella and himself, he motioned for his guards to follow him inside.

They were the only people in the room.

He glared at Emin who grimaced back at him.

"It's hard to keep her safe when she is trained just as well or better than any of us. It looks like she left you a present." Dhamar fingered the video and sound scrambler device before he picked up a small box containing a micro-ear piece.

"She went in alone and never came out," Emin swore.

All exterior doors were still locked. Tarek frowned and tightened his grip on the handle of his cane. Dhamar offered the jeweler's box to him, and Tarek removed the ear piece from it. Inserting it into his left ear, he closed his eyes and breathed deeply before he spoke.

"Idella, where are you?" he asked in a deceptively calm voice.

"There is a pair of sunglasses on the end table. Put them on."

He spotted them where she said they were, walked over, and put them on. Surprise washed through him when a video appeared showing a dark corridor somewhere in the palace. With a curse, he pulled them off and stared at them for a second before he put them on again.

"I'm not sure I want to know where you picked up this little toy. Something tells me you can't buy it at the local market."

Her husky chuckle whispered through the ear piece and sent a bolt of need straight to his groin. How could one woman affect him so powerfully?

"How was your after-dinner drink conversation?" she inquired.

Immediately, his desire cooled. "Kaffir offered to give me Anderson Coldhouse in exchange for you."

This time, it was her rough curse that rang in his ear.

"Well, that might get us Coldhouse a little faster, but I'd have to kill Kaffir when he tried to touch me."

"I threatened to kill him too. Will you tell me how you managed to get out of the room without Emin seeing you?"

She laughed again. He vaguely wondered if she was trying to drive him mad with frustration or insane with desire. Either way, he had every intention of making her scream the next time they had real privacy and enough time to make the best of it.

"The palace is riddled with the coolest network of secret passages. It would appear that the royal family's ancestors were paranoid—for good reason, it turns out. Fortunately, it appears Kaffir never got the memo about them."

Tarek didn't like that, not at all.

"This situation is too dangerous. I think it would be better to abort," he growled.

"I can't. This has become personal. Coldhouse needs to be stopped once and for all."

"Yes, he does, but not now, Idella. We are vastly outnumbered. Kaffir is suspicious."

"I'm always outnumbered, Tarek. This is nothing new," she murmured.

"Come back to me," he quietly requested.

"I will. Soon."

He pulled the glasses off and pinched the bridge of his nose. Feelings of frustration and helplessness coursed through him. The emotions were so foreign to him that he didn't know how to deal with them. He held the glasses out to Emin who took them, put them on, and released a low whistle of appreciation.

"Would you like a drink?" Dhamar asked.

Tarek gave a sharp nod. He kept the ear piece in, wanting to hear Idella if she needed him. Grasping his drink, he settled into the chair.

Dhamar sank into the chair across from him. "I know we've said it before, but I'll say it again. She is a remarkable woman."

"You have no idea," he replied with a rueful smile.

Seventeen

The room was dark when Idella slipped through the secret passage back into the bedroom two hours later. Frustration burned through her. Coldhouse was nowhere to be found. It was as if he had vanished from the palace.

"Innovative," Tarek's quiet voice greeted upon her entry.

She stiffened before relaxing. "It is. The engineer deserves a medal. Even inside them, they can be tricky."

Tarek stepped into a sliver of moonlight coming in through the window. All he wore was a pair of black exercise trousers that sat low on his hips, but his state of undress couldn't distract her from the glitter of anger in his eyes.

"Tarek...." She knew this was coming from a place of fear and worry, she just didn't know how to help.

He stood ridged, his shoulders stiff and his mouth pursed. She walked over to him, and as she slid her hands up his chest, she felt the first flash of fear for their relationship. Harlem had always warned Idella and Raja that people like them were never meant for a happy ever-after. Others just could not understand who they really were—or accept them.

A shudder ran through Tarek's body and he roughly pulled her into his arms. She closed her eyes as tears burned and threatened to spill over. Her heart was pounding and she wound her arms around his neck. They stood in silence, each absorbing the other.

"I love you," she murmured.

It was the first time she had said the words out loud to him—or anyone else. She had never even said the words to Raja or Harlem for fear that it would somehow curse them. The only person she had ever confessed her love to had died in a dark alley on a hot July night. Loving her mother hadn't saved the woman, and after Harlem's warnings, she had buried the words deep inside her.

Tarek's hand threaded through her hair and he gently pulled her head back far enough that he could see her eyes in the moonlight. She poured every ounce of her love into her expression. He crushed his lips to hers in a kiss that rocked her soul, muting her surprised cry.

Her fingers scraped his scalp and their tongues tangled as he silently demanded that she surrender to him. He was a man who had shed his polished, sophisticated exterior, and the primal way he wanted her was an inferno.

It thrilled her. She thought she might combust. His hands slid down her sides, his strong fingers molding the curves of her hips. He swallowed her cries of need and pushed her back against the wall with a hoarse curse. He pulled her shirt over her head, and when he caught sight of her sports bra, he scowled.

"This should be against the law," he muttered.

Idella laughed before she leaned forward to tease his lips. "Take it off me then. Make me naked, and take me to bed."

He groaned, gripped the bottom of the offending piece of material, and pulled it over her head.

She bit his earlobe and playfully said, "The bed, by the way, is optional."

Her suggestive laughter as she toed off one of her boots was interrupted by her gasp of surprise when he scooped her up in his arms.

"Your leg!" she hissed.

"My leg is fine. It is a different part of me that you should be worried about."

She threaded her fingers through his hair. "Your mind?" she teased.

"What's left of it."

Her teasing retort was lost as he tumbled her on the bed and quickly removed the rest of their clothes. If she ever had any doubt that she belonged to Tarek—heart, body, and soul—he vanquished them with a passion that shocked her to the core.

Anderson Coldhouse sipped on the exquisite whiskey in the squat crystal tumbler he had poured from Kaffir's personal bar. He ignored Kaffir's heated glare at his familiarity as he savored the fragrant aroma of caramel, vanilla, and other spices. Pain radiated through his body, a constant reminder of the damage done when the boat exploded. It was a good reminder. He would inflict the same damage on his enemies.

"I'm going to kill Tarek Saif-Ad-Din," he calmly stated.

Kaffir's mouth tightened. "I don't care, just don't do it in the palace. The last thing I need is a declaration of war."

Anderson chuckled and drank more before he spoke. "And the woman?" he asked.

"Idella must remain unharmed. Her international visibility is higher than even the Saif-Ad-Din royal family. If she were to be injured or killed while on Simdan soil, the negative impact could last a long time."

"In other words, you want the bitch," Anderson chuckled with a lift of his glass.

"She is... interesting," Kaffir acknowledged.

Anderson raised an eyebrow. "Do you really think a beautiful, talented, successful woman like that would be interested in *you*?"

Kaffir's eyes narrowed but he didn't reply. Perhaps he was too furious to speak. That only heightened Anderson's enjoyment. There was little Kaffir could do, not without upsetting the connections Anderson had —or risking Anderson turning on him.

"She *will* be mine. Be careful, Coldhouse. You are a guest in *my* country and I am the one who rules it. My sources have informed me that Bronislav is not happy with you. You have failed too many times."

Anderson's eyes glittered with malice. This was suddenly seeming like a setup, and it sure looked like Kaffir needed to die. Healing scabs from his burns made his skin itch, and his fingers were twitching with the need for violence.

"What do you know about Bronislav?" Anderson demanded.

This time it was Kaffir whose smile twisted with a devious pleasure. Anderson's brain was buzzing with warning, the same warning that had saved his life time-and-time again.

"Do you think I was not aware of Bronislav's plan to start a war between Simdan and Jawahir? A war that Simdan would have no chance of winning in its current state. Colin's forces would not be enough to deter the Jawahir Royal Military. Not only that, the international outrage and support would be in Jawahir's favor.

"I will not be anyone's scapegoat, Coldhouse. *Simdan* will not be anyone's scapegoat. You and your brother have outstayed your welcome. If you want to kill the Saif-Ad-Din family, you will do it in Jawahir or somewhere else. You have twelve hours to get out of my country."

"You might regret me leaving, Kaffir," Anderson sneered, setting his empty glass down and rising to his feet.

Kaffir rose as well and lifted his chin with a look of disdain. "I can think of nothing that would make me regret such an act, Mr. Coldhouse."

"Not even the knowledge that Raja Hadi is still alive?"

"Where do you think you are going?" Tarek demanded, looping his arm around Idella and dragging her back to bed.

Idella's smothered giggle sent a bolt of heated blood straight to his groin. He pressed his hand against her mound under the covers, and her giggle turned to a moan of need.

"I'd say you two need to get a room, but... well, you two are in a room," an amused voice stated.

Tarek cursed and pulled the bedspread up to cover them. Idella sighed and shifted onto her back. She caressed his cheek.

"I was going to warn you," she murmured.

He sat up and scowled at the woman sitting in a corner chair. Midnight had one leg thrown over the arm of it and was staring up at the ceiling as if fascinated with the decorative molding.

"What are you doing in our bedroom?" he demanded.

Midnight grimaced. "Yeah, this was not the best place to meet up with you. I'll be in the other room. I've got some info."

With an elegant roll, she stood up and strode out of the room. At least she had the courtesy to shut the door behind her. Tarek fell back against the pillow with a huff.

"How long was she there?" he grumbled, suddenly feeling like a teenage boy caught with his pants down—except *worse* because he was a full-grown man and he had no pants at all.

"Less than a minute," she soothed.

Idella rolled onto her side and slid her hand down his flat stomach. He grabbed her hand to stop her from going lower.

"I'm not sure I like your friends," he muttered.

She straddled him. Her eyes twinkled with amusement, her lush lips curved into a tantalizing smile, her hair a wild mane. He had never seen a more beautiful woman in his life.

"They grow on you," she promised before leaning down to give him a teasing kiss. She had no pants on either, which was very distracting as they aligned just right.

She slipped out of his arms and scrunched her nose at him when he growled again. As she headed for the bathroom, he tossed the covers back, grabbed his trousers, and followed her. Ten minutes later, they both emerged.

Midnight was enjoying samples from different covered dishes. She lifted several delicate pastries onto a plate and settled in the chair in the corner. Her leg was thrown nonchalantly over the arm of the chair and was swinging back and forth while she ate.

"S'not poisoned," she mumbled around the flaky crust in her mouth.

"How can you be sure?" Tarek inquired.

He poured himself and Idella a cup of coffee. Idella murmured her thanks and sank down into a chair by the table. She filled her plate.

"'Cause I made sure. I raided the kitchen myself," Midnight replied, wiping her mouth under her bandana with the back of her hand.

"You said you have some info?" Idella mused, sipping the strong coffee.

Midnight nodded and told them about the meeting between Anderson and Kaffir.

"Have you told Raja?" Idella asked with alarm.

"Yeah, as he was leaving. He said he needed to meet with someone and asked me to tell you to be careful."

Idella's eyelashes lowered to conceal her expression.

"Raja Hadi was here?" he asked.

Idella nodded. "Yes, I saw him last night."

He cursed under his breath. Midnight chuckled and rose to her feet. She stretched her arms above her head and rolled her shoulders.

"I'm beat. I'm going to grab a few hours of sleep. I figure between you, Tarek, and his two goons, you guys can cover things for a while. I'll be around later—not that you'll see me."

She strode for the door and pulled it open. Dhamar jerked to the side with a frown when Midnight exited the room with a little wave of her fingers. Tarek shook his head at Dhamar's glowering expression.

Pulling his attention away from Midnight's departure and Dhamar's self-disgust for not catching her sneaking in, he walked over to the window. The sound of china-on-china was barely discernible. He sensed more than heard Idella coming up behind him.

"I would have told you Raja was here. I... was a little distracted when I returned last night."

"This situation is becoming too volatile, Idella."

She gently tugged on him until he faced her. Her eyes were soft with regret, but determined. It scared the hell out of him that he cared about her more than any person he had ever known.

She ran her hands up his chest. "You're right, it is. I would feel better if you and your men left. Midnight will ensure my band and crew get out safely. This is something I have to finish, Tarek. It is better that I do it without distractions."

He stiffened. A nerve throbbed at his temple. She reached up to soothe it, but he pulled away from her, outraged by her suggestion.

"You aren't the only one that is experienced in this type of situation."

"Tarek, I didn't mean— Damn it, this is why Harlem always cautioned us about getting involved!" She turned away from him and straightened into a stubborn stance. "I have a mission to complete. You do what you have to, but be aware, I will, too."

Idella marched back to their bedroom. Tarek's stomach had a cold knot in it. He knew part of it was rage, but the larger part was fear. He could lose her through death. He could lose her when she finished the mission and left him.

He was dealing with a woman as capable as he was. Breathing deeply, he knew he needed to clear his mind. For both of their sakes, he needed to separate his personal feelings from his professional ones. It was just so damn hard whenever he thought of the Coldhouse brothers, Kaffir, and Bronislav. They would show no mercy to Idella if she fell into their hands.

He strode across the room. Pulling the door open, he nodded to Dhamar and Emin. Perhaps the only way to protect Idella was to do as she suggested.

"Where are we going?" Dhamar inquired in a low voice.

"Home," he replied.

Emin shot him a look of surprise. "Are you serious?"

Tarek flashed a sharp glare. "Of course not, but Kaffir, and most importantly, Coldhouse won't know that."

Eighteen

Needed to take care of a few things. Will
return. Be safe.

Idella read the text message from Tarek a dozen times with disbelief
and apprehension. She rubbed her chest and was dismayed to see her
fingers were trembling.

"Hey, is everything alright?" Chia asked.

Idella looked up and nodded. Her throat felt swollen and she wasn't
able to answer right away. She turned and picked up a cable that
needed to be attached to one of the speakers.

"Yes, have you checked the instruments?" she finally asked.

"Calvin did. Everything's a go. I'll be glad when this gig is done. This
place really gives me the creeps. There are like… armed guards everywhere. Even Ty and Calvin are getting serious bad vibes. Midnight, on
the other hand, has been like a ghost in a cemetery. I'm glad she is on
our side. Where's Tarek and his dastardly duo? That Dhamar guy is
hot. I was hoping he would ask me to play *him*, if you know what I
mean."

"They had to return to Jawahir unexpectedly."

Chia gave her a startled look before shrugging. "Well, that sucks, but I guess a prince has to do what a prince has to do."

"Yes… he does," she softly responded.

"Idella, show is in an hour!" Ty called out. "There is a dressing room set up for you through that door. Midnight has your wardrobe ready."

Idella lifted a hand to show that she heard and handed the cable she'd picked up to Calvin. She walked across the ballroom floor, weaving between the elegant tables. Servants moved around the room, completing the final touches.

She pushed open the door and stepped into a large room with dark red velvet drapes and gold leaf crown molding. A massive marble fireplace dominated one wall. The furniture indicated this room was usually used as a conference room or a lounge area, but there were recent additions for Idella's use: a vanity table and stool, a modesty screen, and a rack that held a dozen beautiful gowns.

"I cleaned the room. Their IT guys were not happy when I 'accidentally' began ripping out their tech."

Midnight held up a small box filled with cameras and microphones, and Idella nodded. She activated the scrambler device in her pocket and placed it on the table before she walked over to the rack of gowns. As she ran her fingers across them, she thought of Tarek.

"Are you okay?" Midnight asked.

Idella nodded. "Yes. Everything is fine."

Midnight scoffed. "You need to work on your *'fine'* look," she said, circling her index finger in front of Idella's face. "It isn't working."

Idella vehemently cursed, using a string of words that had Midnight lifting one delicate eyebrow in surprise. Taking a deep breath, Idella yanked a red satin gown off the rack and glared around the room. There wasn't even a bathroom in here.

"This is the last damn time I perform here," she growled.

Midnight snickered.

The door opened suddenly, and both women turned with a glare of disapproval. While Idella schooled her expression into something slightly more polite, Midnight stepped in front of her and crossed her arms.

"No one but staff is allowed in Idella's changing room while she is getting ready."

"Watch your tone, woman, or I'll cut your tongue out," Kaffir's bodyguard ordered.

His build was that of a miniature linebacker, but Midnight looked him over and scoffed. Kaffir was ignoring the exchange between Midnight and his guard while he stared at Idella.

"Zulfirquar, is there something you need?" she asked in a serene tone.

"I was informed that Prince Saif-Ad-Din has returned to Jawahir with his bodyguards," he said.

Idella stepped behind the modesty screen and tossed the red gown over the top of it. She quickly undressed, tossing each piece seductively over the edge of the screen. She could almost imagine Midnight's jaw hitting the ground.

"Leave us," Kaffir ordered.

Midnight shook her head. "I'm Idella's bodyguard. You and frat boy here can wait for her outside," she coolly replied.

Idella bit back a groan as she pulled the red gown on. Midnight was going to infuriate the men which would lead to the women killing the both of them which would lead to *many* political problems. She stepped out from behind the screen with an apologetic expression on her face. She hoped it was more believable than her *'fine'* expression from earlier.

"Midnight, can you do a final scan of the ballroom and check on the band for me... please," Idella requested.

Midnight's eyes narrowed. Idella could imagine the woman's mouth pursing with displeasure. Still, it was better than having a blood-bath moments before she was expected to perform. One did not kill the leader of a country—even if he deserved it—without an exit strategy.

"Whatever you say, boss. Come on, dog pile. If I've got to leave, so do you," Midnight growled in a low tone.

Kaffir's bodyguard muttered a dire warning that made Midnight laugh. Idella gave up trying to hide her amusement. The man might be bigger and stronger, but if she were to place a bet on a battle between the two, Midnight would win hands down.

"Would you be so kind as to zip me up now that I don't have my staff to help me?" she requested, walking over and turning her back to Kaffir.

Kaffir's beefy fingers curved along her hip in a possessive grip. Idella ground her teeth together, but otherwise showed no reaction. Kaffir pulled the zipper up, making sure she could feel his knuckles running up along her spine as he did so.

I am so going to need a shower after this, she thought with a sigh.

She walked over to the vanity table and sank down on the stool. She could see Kaffir in the reflection of the mirror and quickly looked away from the lascivious glaze in his eyes, focusing instead on styling her hair into an elegant chignon. She pinned it with a series of diamond pins.

"I have something for you to wear," Kaffir said. His wheezing voice was deeper.

Idella finished her hair and began touching up her makeup as he pulled a wide case from the pocket of his robes. He opened the case and placed it on the vanity table. Her breath caught at the sparkling diamond necklace inside. The necklace fell in a series of descending diamond tiers, coming to a center point with a teardrop diamond that had to be at least twenty carats. The set included matching pendant diamond earrings.

"This… is… breathtaking," she murmured, fingering the priceless set.

"It has been in the Simdan royal family for over four hundred years. It was given to the Sheikha by the King on their wedding day," Kaffir explained.

"He must have loved her very much," she said, pulling her hand away.

"I wish for you to wear this tonight. Something so beautiful should be worn by a woman equally as stunning," Kaffir murmured.

"I would be honored," she replied.

Kaffir picked the necklace up and placed it around her neck. Idella smiled at him in the mirror and picked up each of the earrings. The entire set was surprisingly light considering the number and size of the diamonds.

"So beautiful," Kaffir said, brushing his fingers against her neck.

The set did look fantastic against her dark skin. Her dark brown hair and the red satin dress accented the sparkle. She ran her fingers over the teardrop diamond and wondered if Raja's mother ever wore the necklace. She rose from her seat and deftly stepped out of reach.

"I need to warm up my vocal cords before performing. I hope you understand. It is important to prevent damaging them," she said.

"I would love a private performance."

Idella smiled gently as she shook her head. The only 'private performance' she would ever give him would involve slitting his throat.

"It is necessary to do this without distractions. I will not take chances with my health."

She laid her hand on his arm and firmly guided him to the door. Once he was standing on the other side of the threshold, she partially closed the door to allow him one last parting remark.

"I look forward to your performance," Kaffir said with a disgruntled expression.

Idella bowed her head and shut the door.

Leaning her head against it, she closed her eyes. Sometimes she wished she could just kill the fucking bastards of the world and get it over with. She had better things she could be doing with her time.

Tears burned the back of her eyes as she thought of Tarek. She ran a hand over her churning stomach. Her last words to him had been so cold and hateful. She trembled at the thought of never seeing him again—or worse, seeing him and finding out that he no longer wanted her. She opened her eyes and stared at the empty room.

"What have I done?" she whispered.

Earlier

Outside Dima

Tarek sat in the shadows cast by the awning of a café. The street was busy with children begging for money amidst cars, buses, delivery vehicles, motorbikes, and pedestrians. Dust veiled the area, almost as choking as the exhaust fumes.

A man close to Tarek's height with a build that was leaner and wirier sat down in the chair across from him. His clothing was similar to Tarek's except for the headdress that covered his face. Tarek's head-dress was looser, bunching beneath his chin. Sunglasses hid both men's eyes.

Almost immediately, a server set another mug on the table. Steam wafted from the contents. It was the rich aroma of coffee.

"I'm glad you came," Tarek greeted.

Raja Hadi gave a brief nod and pulled the fabric covering his mouth loose so he could sip his brew. "You have four men with you," he said, his voice deep and his tone casual. "Are you sure that is enough?"

Tarek nonchalantly picked up his mug with his left hand, cradled the coffee with both hands, and set it down with his right hand, the signal informing his men that Raja was aware of them but there was no immediate danger.

Raja gave a small smile, his eyes knowing.

Tarek inclined his head in acknowledgement.

"Does Idella know you are still in the country?" the long-lost sheikh of Simdan asked.

"No."

Raja lifted an eyebrow. "If you hurt her, I will kill you," he said coolly, turning his head toward where Adel was positioned with his sniper rifle.

Tarek narrowed his eyes. "Hurting her is the last thing I want."

Raja returned his attention to Tarek, the eye contact direct but relaxed. "Good. I helped saved your life once. Don't make me regret it," he said softly.

"*You* were ready to let me die in the desert."

"Yes."

He waited for Raja to say more, but he didn't. Tarek gritted his teeth. "Do you love her?" he demanded.

Again, Raja lifted an eyebrow. "Do you?"

"Yes," Tarek replied.

The silence dragged on for a few moments. Raja placed his coffee cup on the table and relaxed back in his seat. A wry smile curved the man's lips. "There may be hope for you yet," he said.

Tarek considered that response, wondering again about their relationship. Idella thought of him as a brother, but that did not mean Raja felt the same. He decided to offer a truth, hoping to receive one in return. "I don't like her being in danger," he groused.

Raja threw his head back and laughed.

"What do you find so amusing?" he demanded.

"You—if you think 'not liking' her being in danger will make any difference."

Tarek scowled and Raja went back to observing each of Tarek's hidden men, still chuckling a little. "She would be the most concerned about Butrus," Raja said absently. "He is the one most like us—unpredictable, born on the streets, not quite… tame. Did he make a move on her yet?"

Tarek grimaced. "Yes. She didn't kill him, but there was a moment when, I confess, I was worried."

Raja smiled. "Did she draw blood?"

Tarek hid a smile of his own and cleared his throat. "The reason I requested this meeting was not just to talk about Idella. I would like your assistance getting back into the palace unseen."

Raja paused. Tarek tried to guess what the other man was thinking. There was very little information about Hadi—at least, anything current. It was as if he had dropped off the planet after his family was murdered.

"Why did you pretend to leave the country?" Raja asked.

"Idella…." Tarek placed his cup on the table and leaned forward. "She refuses my assistance."

Raja sighed. "You are going to give it to her anyway."

He sat back with a sharp nod. "She isn't invincible, and she thinks she is. Your uncle has his eye on her. You *know* how cruel he can be."

"Yes. I know."

They were quiet for a moment while he waited for Raja to speak again.

"You realize that if you are discovered, it will cause an international scandal."

Tarek crossed his arms, his expression mulish.

Raja gave an exasperated laugh. "Idella won't be alone, I assure you."

Tarek scoffed. "If *you* are caught, it would be worse. You are the rightful heir to the Simdan throne."

Raja's smile was bittersweet. "I suppose we are in agreement then. We will not abandon her to do this alone… no matter the cost."

Nineteen

Tarek and his men quietly followed Raja through the maze of ancient sewer tunnels. The style of the passages changed, showing architecture from different time periods of Simdan history as they arrived directly beneath the palace. Raja paused abruptly and held up his hand.

The rest of the group did too, waiting silently as conversation filtered down from above, getting quieter as the people above them moved on. Raja gave a brief jerk of his head before he continued walking, and they entered a section that divided into eight passages.

Raja stopped again and turned to face them. Tarek was glad the man was with them. Otherwise, it could take years for them to find their way out.

"Now I know what a rat feels like in a maze," Dhamar muttered.

Raja smirked. "You wouldn't believe how many skeletons I found down here when I was a kid."

Emin and Dhamar looked around them with an uneasy expression. Butrus and Adel turned until they were back-to-back, their weapons pointed toward the ground but at the ready. Tarek ignored them.

"We'll split up here," Raja said. "A two-man team will take tunnels three and five. Tunnel three, you'll want to keep to the right. Tunnel five, keep to the left. You'll each pass four tunnels. Exit it at the fifth. You'll find a staircase that will lead to a trapdoor. Climb the ladder. Near the top, there is a stone drain. You'll have to crawl one hundred feet before you get to the access panel. You'll come out in the ballroom.

"Tunnel three comes out in the front, above the stage. Tunnel five opens onto a small balcony on the second level above the ballroom floor. The space is filled with excess chairs. Unless they need more, you should be able to conceal yourself. You can also use the chairs to block the door and escape back into the tunnels."

"What happens if we have to come back down here and get lost?" Dhamar inquired.

Raja ruefully smiled. "You better hope either Midnight finds you or I don't get killed."

"Great," Butrus muttered.

"Tarek, you'll come with me," Raja said.

Butrus opened his mouth to argue, but Tarek held up his hand and silenced the man. Butrus grunted and nodded.

"Idella's official itinerary is doing a short performance, stopping for dinner, doing another performance, then socializing. Coldhouse will pick the most dramatic moment to attack. He'll want to let Kaffir know that he doesn't give a fuck about what he wants and he'll want to start an international incident just like Bronislav paid his brother to do. Believing Tarek is out of the country, his best chance to do that is by targeting Idella. The whole point is the message. The more witnesses, the better. He'll attack during the show. We have approximately an hour to locate Coldhouse and take him out."

"Where does Tarek fit in?" Emin asked.

Tarek answered slowly. "I'm going to divert attention from Idella. I will be the bait, instead of her."

Raja grinned and nodded. The four men surrounding them frowned and complained.

Tarek chuckled. "She'll want to kill us both if she finds out what we are doing."

Raja laughed and nodded. "I'm counting on you to convince her not to. While you keep her safe, I'll hunt down Coldhouse and take him out."

"Good luck with that," Butrus mumbled.

"I'll need to change," Tarek said with a wave of his hand to his black combat clothing.

"Midnight has a tux ready for you in Idella's dressing room. You'll be able to enter unnoticed through an access panel. Midnight set a placard reserving your seat at the round table near the stage next to Idella—which also means sitting with Kaffir. Sorry."

Tarek's lip curled with contempt.

"We'd better head out. I can hear people entering the ballroom," Butrus muttered.

Tarek nodded. "If you get a clear shot of Coldhouse, take the hit and get out."

"Yes, sir," Dhamar said with a touch of his fingers to his temple.

Tarek turned to Raja and nodded. "Let's do this."

Idella stepped up to the microphone and smiled. Her red silk dress blazed in the spotlight and her diamonds sparkled. Out of habit, her glance swept over each person in the audience, categorizing them into the threat or not-a-threat column before scanning the rest of the room for any risks. Her eyes briefly paused on the upper-level balconies.

Was there a movement in the shadows? she wondered.

S.E. SMITH

She turned away, her eyes connecting with Midnight. The woman lifted the thumb on her right hand, pointing upward. There was no alarm in Midnight's eyes. No, the expression was more like... amusement... satisfaction?

Idella twisted as if she were communicating with Chia and tilted her head back far enough to look up above the stage. Her eyes connected with a pair of familiar, intense brown eyes—Butrus. Chia began the intro to her latest hit song.

Turning to face the audience, Idella pulled the microphone free from the stand at the same instant that Tarek sat down in an empty place setting next to the spot reserved for her. Only her lifelong training kept her from showing that his appearance had an effect on her.

He looked devastatingly handsome in that tux. Something wicked unfurled inside her and when she began to sing, she directed the full force of her passion to him. In her mind's eye, she undressed him, and she reveled in the delicious heat that she felt from the top of her head to her curling toes.

Her sultry voice and subtle, sensual dancing mesmerized men and women alike in the audience. The temperature in the room elevated. By the time she finished the song, more than one woman in the audience was fanning themselves while the men tried to adjust their seating without being too obvious.

Tarek's eyes were blazing with desire and the promise of retribution. Idella had to turn away to take a sip of water. She felt like living flame, and she imagined burning this whole place down as she consumed him.

"What the fuck was that?" Ty hoarsely demanded.

Calvin nodded. "Damn, Idella. I swear every guy in the room has either jacked-off under the table or is about to. I'm about ready to bust a load and I've heard you sing that damn song a million times," he choked.

Chia shook her head. "Pussies. I hope that sensuality comes through on the video feed. It'll go viral," she exclaimed with delight.

"Let's hit the next song while I have everyone enthralled," Idella said.

"Double *damn*! This is going to be a long night," Calvin laughed. "If only Chia and Midnight would help me relieve the pain...." he added forlornly, a twinkle of mischief in his eyes as he looked at Chia from beneath his lashes.

"Keep dreaming, Calvin. If I had my way, I'd show you the different levels of *purgatory* in your dreams," Chia retorted with a roll of her eyes.

"Oh, kinky," Ty teased. "Does it involve chains and whips?"

"Here we go," Idella interrupted before turning back to the audience.

Idella flashed one of her mysterious smiles to the crowd and began singing her next song. She looked at the front table long enough to keep Kaffir's attention locked on her before she continued scanning the room. She didn't miss that Tarek was doing the same thing.

There. No one else in the world would have noticed her slight stiffening or the brief flash of anger in her eyes before she concealed it. Only Tarek and Raja knew her well enough to know that her mindset had switched from sultry, international singing sensation to cold-blooded assassin who had found her target.

Anderson Coldhouse was standing near the huge double doors. Butrus's line of sight would be obstructed. Whoever was in the balcony would never see Anderson standing below them. The only one with a clear line of sight were those on the stage—and from the smug expression on Anderson's face, he knew it.

She finished the last song in the first session of her performance. The audience rose like a wave, blocking her view of Anderson. By the time they sat down again, Anderson was gone. The bitter taste of having her target so close and then gone made her stomach churn.

Her gaze flashed to Kaffir. Raja's uncle was still standing and enthusi-astically clapping. His eyes were roaming over her as if he were strip-ping the clothes off of her in front of everyone. She forced her eyes away from him to Tarek. A frown creased her brow when she saw that he, too, was gone. Scanning the room, she caught sight of him as he exited the ballroom. The sickening churn in her stomach exploded into a full-body alarm, and for a moment, she almost forgot who she was supposed to be.

"You did great," Midnight murmured near her ear. "Take a time out and keep Kaffir and his henchmen distracted. I'll make sure his prince-liness is safe."

"Be careful," she said.

Midnight tilted her head, mockingly lifting her eyebrow as if she were offended, and disappeared behind the curtain of the stage. The rest of the band was dispersing for the scheduled break. Idella breathed deeply.

"A magnificent performance, *eazizi,*" Kaffir replied.

Idella ignored the endearment. "Thank you."

Kaffir's lips tightened when he noticed her looking towards the door-way. He gripped her elbow and guided her to the chair next to his. She frowned when his fingers squeezed hard enough to bruise.

"I was not expecting Sheikh Tarek's return," Kaffir said.

Idella tugged her arm free as she sank down onto the chair. "I wasn't aware that he was returning either," she coolly replied.

"A shame that he did. This… complicates matters a bit," Kaffir said.

Idella was about to ask him to clarify his remark when a server approached and placed a dish in front of her. She murmured a thank you. It took every ounce of discipline in her to remain seated and not search the room for Tarek's men. Surely, they knew he had left the dining room?

Idella stiffened when Kaffir caressed her thigh under the table. She gripped his wrist, applying enough pressure on a nerve that his hand opened and he pulled it away. She stared at him with an expression of distaste.

"I don't like being touched without giving permission first," she stated in a cold voice.

Kaffir rubbed his wrist and sneered at her. "I look forward to receiving your permission... very soon."

Idella slipped her hand under the table and fingered the sheathed ultra-thin blade strapped to her thigh. It would be so tempting to open Kaffir up and leave him bleeding.

Soon, she silently promised herself. *Very, very soon.*

Twenty

The muscle in Tarek's jaw throbbed as he made his way back to the ballroom. He had lost Coldhouse in the maze of corridors. When two of Kaffir's henchmen suddenly blocked his path, Tarek was very tempted to take out his frustration on them. He was so tired of being surrounded by threats and refusing to fight for the sake of avoiding war.

He was warily eyeing the corridor behind them, assessing his options, when Midnight suddenly appeared beside him. She stepped between him and the men and straightened his bowtie like she did it every day.

"You already know this, but Kaffir's up to something," she murmured near his ear before turning to face the two men. "The Prince was kind enough to help me look for the bathrooms, but I swear I haven't found anything resembling one in this mausoleum. Can either of you stone statues point me in the direction of the little girls' room?" she asked in a bright, faux-cheerful voice.

The henchmen folded their arms and stared at her in silence. Midnight raised an eyebrow and shrugged.

"Okay, well, I guess I'll just go find a cup or a bush or something," she retorted, turning on her heel. "There obviously are no bathrooms this way, Your Highness."

She threaded her arm through his and pushed her way between the two henchmen. Tarek realized Midnight was guiding him back to the ballroom. The two guards followed them in stony silence. He was surprised when Midnight brushed her palm against his. Her hand wasn't empty. He took the knife.

"Idella will begin her next performance in five minutes," Midnight murmured.

Tarek nodded, silently wondering if his body could handle another performance like the first one. It had taken all of his willpower not to snatch Idella off the stage, throw her over his shoulder, and carry her into the desert for the next fifty years so he could have her safe and all to himself. He was done with dealing with the likes of Coldhouse, Bronislav, and Kaffir.

Instead, he was forced to grit his teeth and slide into the empty chair across from Kaffir as Idella walked onstage with a sexy sway of her hips. Kaffir eyed him with an assessing, almost gleeful expression. He kept his own eyes glued on Idella as she began singing.

Let the second round of torture begin, he mused with an almost savage pleasure.

Two guards stood by the door of Idella's dressing room. On the other side of the door, Idella's voice mesmerized the audience with her wide vocal range and the magic of the lyrics. Inside the room, Anderson smirked at the bloody man that had a hangman's noose pulled taut around his throat. Dressed all in black, his arms tied behind his back, he stood on the vanity stool, his mouth covered with a thick piece of silver duct tape.

"My brother discovered the tunnel system not long after your uncle took over the palace," Anderson chuckled. "He wasn't successful in mapping all of it, but enough to move around undetected. A brilliant feat of engineering, wouldn't you agree, Hamlet? Or should I call you Raja Hadi, the rightful ruler of Simdan?" He sneered, the motion pulling on the scar tissue on his face.

The man kept his unusual navy-blue eyes locked on him, but not a single ounce of emotion showed. Anger burned inside Anderson. Remembering the agony he had gone through while chasing all these worthless ants, he needed Raja Hadi to feel—he wanted to revel in the other man's pain.

He pulled a pocketknife out of his front pocket and flicked it open. The steel blade glinted in the bright light of the room. Raja's expression didn't change, but it would soon. Anderson smiled.

He lifted the blade at the same time the door behind him opened. The masked woman froze at the entrance, Idella's music streaming in with her as she took in the scene.

"What the fu—"

"Get her," Anderson ordered.

Instead of running screaming for help, the woman dropped to the floor as the two guards reached for her and quietly closed the door—with her inside the room. The woman swiveled in a tight circle, both arms outstretched, her knives glinting in the light. The guards fell back with shocked expressions on their faces, their hands going to their stomachs. Before they could stumble out of her reach, the woman rose in a beautiful pirouette, the tips of her long blades slicing through the guards' carotid arteries.

The men were dead before they hit the floor. Anderson whipped around and surged toward Raja, determined to bury his blade in the man's chest. The breath was knocked out of him when Raja tensed his neck muscles against the noose and raised both his legs, driving them into the center of his chest. The blow knocked Anderson off balance and he stumbled backward.

Pain exploded through Anderson when one of the woman's blades pierced his left shoulder. He struck, his pocketknife slicing through the woman's blood-red shirt, missing the tender flesh of her ribcage by the thickness of a spider's silken strand.

The woman's eyes flashed with deadly intent as she advanced on him. Raja's face began to turn red as he hung from his neck while he searched for the stool with his feet. Anderson kicked at the stool. It slid across the floor.

The woman's eyes flickered from the stool, to Raja, and back to Anderson. He had to give her credit. She was actually considering this, as if Raja Hadi's life was worth giving Anderson a better chance to kill them both. He smiled and lifted his hands up.

"What will it be? Me, or him?" he taunted with a jerk of his head.

The woman's muttered curse alerted him she would save Raja. He darted into the hidden tunnels as she lunged for the stool.

So, Raja has a partner who works for the delectable singer.

That knowledge made him realize that he was approaching things from the wrong angle. The masked woman, Raja, and Tarek all had one person in common that they cared about and wanted to protect. If he captured her, he held the golden key.

Gritting his teeth against the pain in his shoulder, he stumbled through the darkness. He needed more men. As much as he hated to admit it, he needed to contact his brother for help.

"Get Chia and the others out of here and onto the plane. I want all of you out of the country within the hour," Idella ordered.

Midnight bowed her head in acknowledgement. "What about Kaffir and Coldhouse?"

Idella breathed deeply before she spoke in a slow, measured tone, "Raja and I will take care of them. I need you to make sure the band is safe."

Midnight looked as if she was about to argue. Raja shook his head. Midnight pursed her lips, turned, and exited the room. The band members were disassembling the equipment and packing it up.

Idella turned her focus to Raja. Dark bruising encircled his throat. She swallowed the bile that roiled up from her stomach and looked down.

"There's still blood on the floor," she observed.

Raja's raw laugh made her heart hurt. "Well, you know Midnight when she plays with her knives," he retorted in a gruff voice.

"I'm supposed to join Kaffir and his associates for after-dinner drinks," she said.

"Tarek's men will help me dispose of the bodies and finish cleaning up. You and Tarek keep Kaffir occupied," Raja said.

"And after that? If Anderson has a map to the hidden tunnels, he could be anywhere!" she snapped.

She pursed her lips. Her emotions were running too close to the surface. Anderson getting the jump on Raja had shaken her foundation. With both Raja's close call and Tarek in danger, she felt like she was about to explode. This was not how missions were supposed to go.

Harlem was right. Loving someone, having these emotions, it only causes distractions. It gets people, innocent people, killed. I can't keep them safe.

"I have a shadow on the inside, following Anderson," Raja assured her. "That's who I met this afternoon... well, one of the people I met. Anderson hasn't disappeared."

Idella stared at him. "Do I know the shadow?"

Raja shook his head. "No... but I trust this person with my life."

A knock at the door made her stiffen. Raja stepped back against the wall when the door opened a crack. It was Midnight.

"We're about to leave. I told Tarek what happened. He's with Kaffir now. The creep insisted he needed to speak with him alone."

"Watch your back and sweep the plane before it takes off," Idella cautioned.

"I will. You might want to check in with Bugs," Midnight replied before pulling back and shutting the door.

Idella closed her eyes and breathed, wondering what else could go wrong tonight. Her eyes popped open when Raja touched her shoulder, his expression concerned.

"I'll check the messages while you change," he said.

She shook her head. "I'll do it. We'll regroup after the party."

Raja gave a brief nod. Moments later, Raja and Tarek's men finished sanitizing the room and she changed into an elegant one-piece black jumpsuit. She added a thick silver chain belt, winding it around her waist three times before sliding the bladed-ends into the latch. She put on twin chain bracelets that could be used as a variety of weapons. Last, she picked up a clutch that had a thin strap. She tested the spool of razor wire that was concealed in the extra-large clasp before exiting the room without a backwards glance.

Two of Kaffir's guards waited behind a roped-off area near the door. Idella suspected that Midnight had placed the barrier there and was surprised that it worked. Midnight gave her a brief nod as Calvin and Ty rolled the equipment out.

The two guards fell in behind her and several servers paused and bowed to her as she walked toward the exit of the ballroom. She took a moment to thank them for their wonderful service. Pride and determination nearly choked her when one young girl handed her a bouquet gathered from the tables.

"One day, when the true king returns, I hope all of our people can hear you sing. It would bring great joy to my people," the girl said in halting English, glancing nervously at the guards.

"Hopefully, that day will come soon," Idella replied, kissing the girl on each cheek before she continued.

An additional guard was waiting at the entrance of the room. She followed him through the corridors and down a staircase. Her steps slowed when he opened the door to a room and she noticed that instead of a crowd of guests, only Tarek, Kaffir, and two of his generals were inside.

General Gamar was notable as he stood stiffly behind Tarek, anger burning in his eyes. The other general's face was a blank mask. Kaffir was smug, and Tarek was calm. Behind her, the three guards stepped inside and closed the door.

"I am pleased that you have joined us," Kaffir greeted in his irritating voice.

Her fingers tightened on her clutch.

"I... must have misunderstood. I thought there was an after-party for a few select guests," she said.

"It's definitely a party," Colin Coldhouse chuckled from the shadows.

Her heart hammered, but Idella forced her expression to indicate confusion. She watched Anderson's older brother step into the dim light and cursed herself for not reading Bugs' message. She was sure it would have warned her that Anderson was no longer the only Coldhouse in the palace.

"Knock him out," Colin ordered.

A cry of denial burst from Idella when Gamar pistol-whipped Tarek. Her rush forward was halted when the guards behind her gripped her arms. She struggled ineffectually, resolved to reveal her skills later at a more opportune moment. There was still a chance that she could talk her way into a better position to strike. Perhaps she could get them to turn against each other and take advantage of their distraction.

"What is going on?" she demanded.

She wrenched her glare from Colin to Kaffir. A pleased smile curved the rotund sheikh's lips and he closed the distance between them. She jolted back a step when he invaded her space.

He hummed with approval. "Let us just say you are worth an international incident, *eazizi*," Kaffir said, lifting his hand to caress her cheek.

Idella turned her face away from the man and closed her eyes. Kaffir would know he was about to be a dead man if she looked at him.

"What... are you going to do with us?" she asked, her voice trembling.

"Now, that is a very interesting question... Idella," Colin replied, staring down at Tarek's inert body.

"I can tell you what we are going to do with her," another voice stated. "We are going to use her to capture Hamlet, Dallas, and finish the job we were hired to do!"

Kaffir cursed and turned with a startled expression. "How did you get in here?" the corpulent sheikh demanded.

"There is a lot about this palace you should have taken more time to learn about," Anderson tossed out before turning to his brother. "I didn't expect you to be here already."

Colin shrugged. "You have information about Dallas and Hamlet?"

Anderson's expression turned smug. "Yes." He turned his attention to Idella. She returned his stare with a cool one of her own. "Dallas is the masked woman who works for Idella as part of her security. It makes sense now how she could get in and out of countries without being noticed."

"Are you sure?" Colin demanded.

Anderson's expression turned almost savage. "I've got a fucking hole in my shoulder from her, and two of Kaffir's guards were dead before they hit the ground. Yeah, I would say I'm pretty sure," he snapped.

"Who is this Dallas and Hamlet?" Kaffir demanded.

Colin's expression turned grim. "My counterparts in the business. Governments hire them to take out people like you and me. Those two have been a pain in my ass for the last three years," he said.

"I would have delivered Hamlet to you on a platter if it hadn't been for that bitch," Anderson commented.

"I don't care," Kaffir growled. "I need you to make Sheikh Tarek's death appear to be an accident. Jawahir *cannot* blame me. The woman stays with me."

Anderson walked over and used the toe of his boot to roll Tarek onto his back. Idella fought a berserker's rage when he kicked Tarek in the side where he had been shot.

"You might want to rethink being so dismissive... especially about Hamlet. You might know him by a different name—Raja Hadi. I believe the people call him the Savior of Simdan," Anderson replied.

Kaffir paled before his face turned beet red. The three generals standing around him drew in hissing breaths.

Colin raised an eyebrow and studied his brother. "Getting that information must have been fun. You look like shit."

Anderson flicked his middle finger up in reply. Idella's mind played out one scenario after another, looking for a way to take out the men in the room without endangering Tarek. No matter how she played it, someone would take Tarek hostage—or worse, kill him while she was distracted and he was helpless.

Kaffir pulled a pistol from his waist and an icy sensation flooded her when he pointed it at Tarek. She rammed her spiked heel into the shin of the guard on her left. Yanking her arm free, she struck the other guard in the throat. The moment she was free, she threw herself over Tarek, shielding his body with her own.

"Please… don't," she begged, a fake sob catching in her throat.

Laying her forehead against Tarek's, she fervently begged him to wake up. She touched his head where Gamar had struck him. There was a knot, but no blood. His lips tenderly brushed against her cheek, and genuine relieved tears burned the back of her eyes.

Bruising fingers wrapped around her upper arm, pulling her away from Tarek. Colin thrust her toward Kaffir who grabbed her around the waist.

"It's hard to make his death look like an accident if he has a bullet in him," Colin dryly commented.

Kaffir muttered in Arabic to the guards. "Take him down to the lower level and lock him up until we are ready to deal with him."

Idella held her breath, counting the seconds until Tarek would be safely tucked away and she could strike. That opportunity faded when Colin pressed his pistol against her temple.

His eyes were on Kaffir, but he spoke to his brother. "Anderson, take the woman with you."

Kaffir's eyes widened with outrage. "I told you she is to stay with me!"

Colin glanced at the Sheikh with disdain. "She's too valuable as bait. Take her," he ordered again. "I'll deal with the Jawahir prince."

Anderson stepped in front of her, gripped her wrists, and bound them together with a plastic strap. She remained still while the cold metal of Colin's gun pressed against her heated flesh.

"Where is your security agent?" Colin asked Idella.

Her gaze collided with Colin's cold brown eyes. "My band should be on my private jet headed back to the States. You don't seriously believe that Midnight is a government agent, do you? She lives in New York and works at my club. Kaffir's guards would have been marshmallows compared to some people she has dealt with on the streets of Harlem."

Doubt flickered in Colin's eyes and he glanced at his brother. "Don't listen to her," Anderson snarled. "I know what I saw, Colin. The woman moved like a professional. Two men, two slashes of a blade, and she didn't run when she saw her partner hanging from a rope. She also debated whether to help him or go after me."

"We'll know the truth soon enough. I have my men combing the palace for Hadi. Once we have him, it will only be a matter of time before Dallas appears. In the meantime, I'll find out what the Jawahir prince knows before he dies in a tragic plane crash," Colin said.

"What about me?" Kaffir demanded. "I'm the Sheikh of Simdan! I'm in charge, and Idella is mine. Give her back."

Colin cruelly laughed. "If we don't get Hadi, you might be more worried about the war that is about to erupt under your ass." He cast a dismissive nod at the three generals who were standing stiffly behind Kaffir. "You might want to get them to do their jobs and let me focus on mine. Get her back to my compound, Anderson, and don't muck it up this time." Colin turned on his heel and exited the room.

Idella stumbled forward on her heels when Anderson roughly pushed her toward the hidden panel, leaving behind Kaffir as he conversed frantically with his generals. A grim smile of satisfaction curled her lips as she stepped into the narrow passage and the panel closed behind Anderson.

Twenty-One

Tarek straightened the cuffs of his tuxedo and stared dispassionately at the two guards sprawled on the ground. He had taken the guards by surprise in the dimly lit corridor beneath the palace.

He still would have been shot by the second guard as he dispatched the first, but fortunately, Emin and Dhamar had appeared before the guard fired.

"How did you know where I was?" he asked.

Dhamar lifted his phone. "Midnight placed a tracking device in your tux," he replied.

"Where are Raja and the others?" he said, gingerly touching the bump on the back of his head.

"Adel is making sure Midnight and the band make it to the airport and take off without incident. Butrus is with Raja. We brought you a change of clothes." Emin held out a small, black duffel bag.

Tarek nodded his thanks, took the bag, and changed into black military cargo pants, a black long-sleeve shirt, and black boots. Dhamar filled him in on what had happened to Raja earlier.

"The tunnels are crawling with men now. They don't look like Kaffir's," Emin added.

Tarek nodded. "Colin Coldhouse is here. He knows about the underground tunnels and hidden passages," he warned.

"That explains the military demeanor and equipment they have," Emin muttered.

"Where's Idella?" Dhamar asked.

Tarek's lips flattened into a grim line. "Anderson has her."

"That's not good—for Anderson," Dhamar retorted with a sardonic smile.

Emin lifted his hand in a clenched fist before touching his index finger to his lips. *We're about to have company,* he mouthed.

Tarek checked the automatic weapon Dhamar handed him and silently nodded. They moved into a three-man defensive position as Colin Coldhouse and several mercenaries rounded the corner. Tarek locked eyes with Colin as the man pulled the nearest mercenary in front of himself and both sides opened fire.

Idella stumbled again when Anderson shoved her in her lower back. She leaned against a stack of crates in the palace loading area and decided this would be a good place to leave his body. She slid her hand to the concealed opening in the material of her jumpsuit, pulled her blade from the sheath, and turned it between her palms as she straightened. It cut through the thick plastic zip-tie easily.

Anderson scanned the empty loading bay, his eyes searching for threats before he turned back to her with a growl. She drove her spiked high heel into the meaty flesh of his thigh, hatred powering her strike. Anderson's eyes widened with shock and he howled in pain, falling onto his back.

A roundhouse kick knocked the pistol out of his hand. It skittered across the landing before toppling over the edge. Anderson gripped his bleeding thigh with one hand and scooted back, staring up at her with outrage.

Idella flashed him one of her famous sultry smiles as she removed one of her high heels and then the other. She held them up by her index fingers before she dropped them one at a time, the delicate shoes clattering against the concrete. She tilted her head to study him with a calm, assessing demeanor, and Anderson's rage banked to a wary confusion.

"You don't know how long I've waited for this moment," she finally said, her hands moving to her waist.

She unlatched her belt. The chain fell in loops around her as she gripped the ornate buckle that looked like a serpent's body. She snapped the chain, and the blades on the end sliced through Anderson's thin shirt, parting the flesh of his upper arm.

Anderson shrieked and rolled to get away from her. She struck again. The blades raked across his body armor before slicing his left buttock. Anderson howled and began inching toward the edge of the platform where his gun had gone over.

"Tsk, tsk, tsk... no body armor there," she commented.

Anderson rolled onto his back and glared up at her. He was leaving a trail of dark red blood as he pushed himself across the concrete loading platform. There would be a lot more of it before she was finished.

"Who are you? You're not just a singer," he said as he reached for the knife at his waist.

She flicked her whip at his hand. Shaking her head, she continued following him. Harlem and Raja would both be furious with her. She knew the rules. 'Never play with your target'. It gave them an opportunity to escape or kill you. It also opened the door for something far darker than being an assassin.

Some rules were made to be stretched, she reasoned.

"You were partially correct earlier," she replied. "Hamlet is Raja Hadi, the Savior of Simdan. Unlike Shakespeare's Hamlet, Raja will have no remorse when he kills his uncle—just as I will have none ridding the world of you."

"You... said I was partially correct. What part did I get wrong?"

She kept her eyes locked on his, anticipating his counter-attack. She flicked the chain again, leaving a bloody path across both of his thighs. Anderson released a choked scream and sat up, clutching his legs. Acid burned in her stomach as she thought of Anderson's victims. Anderson had not given in to their pleas for mercy. Instead, he got high on their cries and drunk on their suffering. She breathed deeply, fighting the soul-deep chill seeping through her body.

"Midnight isn't Dallas, I am. A powerful government has hired me to take you out. The difference between you and my other targets is this has become personal. You shouldn't have messed with my friends. And you really shouldn't have targeted the man I love."

There was death in her eyes. She wanted Anderson to see it—feel it—and he did. Her bloodlust rose, and Harlem's warning screamed through her mind, coating her skin in a clammy glaze of sweat.

"Don't fall over the edge. Whatever happens, don't fall over the edge, baby girl. Don't lose the last bit of your soul. There's no getting it back. Keep your head. Stay cool. Focus on your mission."

Idella slowly shook her head back and forth. Vivid flashes of Tarek lying in a pool of blood in the desert threatened to overwhelm her. She pushed that vision away, focusing instead on his arms wrapped around her in his office, loving her, calming her. She sighed, remembering the taste of Tarek's mouth. Fighting the urge to close her eyes, she shuddered. Tears blurred her vision and she tightened her grip on the whip.

"I won't fall. I won't." The words ripped from her throat. She wouldn't let someone like Anderson drag her over the cliff. She deserved a better life.

She trembled as she threw her knife. The four-inch blade didn't quiver when it struck Anderson between the eyes. His head thudded back against the concrete with a dull crack.

She looked up at the sky and released a shuddering breath.

"I can hear you, Harlem," she growled, wiping away her tears. "I didn't do it for you."

The familiar hum of a military-grade helicopter made her grimace and she stepped back into the shadows of the overhang. Through the open door of the helicopter, Colin Coldhouse stared down at his dead brother.

Where is a missile launcher when I need one? she ruefully mused as the helicopter flew away from the palace.

There would be no finishing this mission until she caught up with Colin and Bronislav. She watched from under the overhang as the helicopter gained altitude and disappeared into the night.

She was turning away when an explosion on the outskirts of the city alerted her that something else was going on. She needed to find Tarek and Raja.

She quickly wound the titanium chain back into a belt and slid the blades back into the intricate clasp, retrieved her knife, cleaned it on Anderson's sleeve, and picked up her shoes. A quick sweep of the area showed no evidence of who killed Anderson.

In seconds, she was following Bugs' tracking signal to Tarek's location. She slipped through a doorway into the underground tunnels as more explosions shook the palace grounds.

The unmistakable stench of death hung in the air.

"What was that?" Adel grumbled, warily surveying the bits of dust raining down on the six men who were finally all in the same place.

"The fight for my country has begun," Raja stated.

"Couldn't you have waited until we weren't in a freaking catacomb before giving the order?" Butrus demanded.

Raja laughed at the growl of annoyance in Butrus's voice. "What fun would that have been?"

"Long time, no see," Idella called before she stepped into view.

"Idella." Tarek breathed her name like a prayer as he strode over to her and pulled her into his arms. He captured her upturned lips in a hard kiss before he pulled back, his eyes roving over her as he looked for injuries. He released a breath of relief when he saw none.

"So, we're having a party in tunnels that might collapse soon. This is fun," she casually observed, glancing around.

His low chuckle chased away the darkness inside her. She scanned the group, and her eyes paused again on the bruising around Raja's neck.

"Colin Coldhouse and his men took off in a helicopter ten minutes ago," she said.

"Where's Anderson?" Raja asked.

She stiffened, a shudder running through her body. At first, she looked haunted, but a moment later her expression softened. Her lips curved in a small, half smile.

"He's dead," she replied.

"You sure?" Dhamar inquired.

She raised an eyebrow at him, and he continued, "Let's face it, the guy has to have gone through at least nine lives by now."

Idella nodded. "I put a knife between his eyes. I guarantee you, he won't be getting back up."

"Sounds good to me. Let's find Kaffir. I'd like to put one between his," Butrus said.

"No." Raja put his hand on Butrus's arm and shook his head. "There can be no links between Jawahir and Simdan. This is my fight now. My forces are taking over the city as we speak. The rest of the country will follow. It is best if all of you are not part of this," he said.

"Raja," Idella murmured with concern.

Raja touched her cheek for a moment before dropping his hand. "Get on your plane and get out of here. We still need to take care of Colin and Bronislav, but I need to save my country first. It can't wait any longer," he said.

"Leave Colin and Bronislav to Qadir and me," Tarek murmured. "We have enough proof to satisfy us. Bronislav was behind the attack on my brother and me. You focus on your uncle. Jawahir needs a strong neighbor."

"May peace be with us soon," Raja said.

Idella watched as Raja disappeared through the tunnels, her heart in her eyes. Tarek held her close, breathing in her intoxicating scent. Another rumble shook the ground, forcing them apart as more bits of rock and dust rained down on them.

"Does anyone know the way out of this death trap?" Adel muttered.

Idella laughed softly and held up her phone. "I do, thanks to a friend."

Twenty-Two

Three weeks later, Tarek entered the tactical command room two levels below his office. The room was filled with some of Jawahir's best logistic officers, military minds, and intelligence analysts.

His brother, Jameel, an elite MIT graduate and computer genius, lifted his hand in greeting before returning his focus on the bank of monitors on the far wall. High-resolution images of Cold Methods Security Compound were displayed on the center screen.

"What is the team's ETA?" he demanded.

"They are in position now," Abdal replied.

Tension rolled off the young tech. Tarek knew that Abdal's sister, Selima, was part of the team going in.

This was a perilous maneuver. The only reason it had been sanctioned was because of his father and Qadir's tireless negotiations with the Lithuanian anti-terrorism division.

"Iceberg, this is Dallas. Final blossoms have been planted."

Tarek breathed deeply when he heard the distorted voice. Jameel looked over his shoulder at Tarek, waiting for a reply.

"Permission to go," Tarek replied.

"Dallas, this is Iceberg, you have permission to go," Jameel replied.

The screen flashed and then the half-dozen buildings that made up Cold Methods Security imploded in clouds of dust. Automatic gunfire could be heard. The satellite feed showed two cargo planes, a small Lear jet, and four helicopters near three hangers. The cargo plane exploded, followed a minute later by the Lear jet and two helicopters. One of the helicopters was lifting off when smoke began pouring out of the fuselage. A moment later, it flew approximately a thousand yards before crashing in a fiery blast.

"Dallas, has the target been neutralized?" Tarek asked.

"Negative. I have a visual. I am going after the target," Dallas replied.

"That is a negative. Let ARAS take over," Tarek ordered, referring to the Lithuanian Police Anti-terrorist Operations Unit that was on site.

Silence greeted him and he muttered a curse. "Jameel, location of Dallas," he ordered.

"On it," Jameel said, eyes flashing from the computer in front of him to the bank of monitors.

Tarek paced back and forth, his eyes on the screens, his headset giving him live updates from several other members of the team. He tried not to flinch every time he heard automatic fire or a muted scream.

"The target is on the move and Dallas is in pursuit," Selima reported.

In the satellite feed he saw five vehicles moving out. He froze. Four in front with one following behind. The image became unstable.

"What's going on? Get the feed back up!" he yelled.

"We're trying. They are moving out of satellite range," Abdal said, his fingers flying over his keyboard.

"They will be over the border in less than 5km. We aren't sanctioned to operate in Belarus," Jameel warned.

"Dallas, watch your track. You have less than 5km to stop the target," Tarek warned.

"Uh-oh," Abdal muttered.

"Dallas, abort," Jameel warned. "Hostile helicopter closing in from the west. I repeat, Dallas, abort your pursuit."

"Ground missile has been launched," Abdal hissed.

"Missile deployment. Hit in ten… nine… eight… seven…"

The vehicle pursuing Coldhouse was hit. Silence descended over the room as the task force watched it explode.

Heart thundering, Tarek pulled off his headset. Dropping it onto the desk, he stared with unseeing eyes.

I should never have agreed to let her go, he numbly thought.

Border with Belarus, southeastern Lithuania:

Idella rolled a dozen times before she finally came to a stop in the overgrown weeds along the dirt and gravel road. She laid on her back, staring up at the blue sky and breathed deeply. Wincing, she pressed one foot to the ground, lifted her left side, and pulled a clump of hard clay from beneath her lower back.

That's better.

She winced again when the ground shook and a loud explosion reverberated. Plumes of black smoke rose into the air.

Overhead, a military-grade Huey Bell UH-1 Iroquois helicopter, straight out of the Vietnam era, passed over her. Thanks to the smoke, the tall grass, and her clothing, the man with the AK47 didn't see her.

She groaned. Colin Coldhouse had escaped again. The only satisfaction was that he no longer had his multi-million-dollar compound and she knew he was injured—badly. His scorched clothing gave it away. If his injuries didn't kill him, seeing his bank account crash and burn along with his international terrorist organization might.

"Iceberg, this is Dallas, target is a no-go. I repeat, the target has escaped," she murmured.

"Dallas, that is an affirmative. Glad to know we aren't picking up pieces. OM requests that you return to base," Jameel said.

"Affirmative, Iceberg," she replied.

She lifted her hand and grinned when she saw the screen on her phone covered in little bugs.

Thank goodness for satellites.

∾

One week later

Colours Nightclub, New York City

Buddy, one of Idella's bouncers, opened the private entrance door for Tarek. Just inside, Midnight was leaning against the wall and motioned for him to follow her. Once on the second floor, she silently bowed her head to him and disappeared. He couldn't help but wonder about the mysterious woman's story as she vanished into the dark recesses of the club.

"Prince Saif-Ad-Din, if you'll follow me, I have your table ready," Karly greeted with a pleasant smile.

Tarek followed the hostess to the same table he remembered from more than three years ago when he first spoke to Idella. He slid into the chair, gave Karly his drink order, and relaxed—until his eyes paused on two familiar men at a table next to him. He glared at them. Dhamar and Emin raised their glasses in acknowledgement before they rose and joined him.

"This place isn't so bad," Butrus commented as he and Adel sat down at his table.

Tarek resisted the urge to scowl at them. Karly returned with his drink and took Butrus and Adel's orders. Tarek paused when he saw Butrus's watchful eyes following Karly. He took a sip of his drink before he said anything.

"I thought I told you that there was no need to join me tonight."

Adel lifted a shoulder and rested his arm along the railing. "Correction. You said 'Take the night off and go have some fun.'"

"And that fun just happens to be here?" Tarek dryly responded.

Butrus grunted, his attention on Karly as she climbed the staircase with his and Adel's fresh drinks. "It's a club, there's entertainment," he said.

"And beautiful women," Adel chuckled.

"Vodka, straight up... and a Scotch and Water, no water," Karly cheerily said.

Butrus reached for Karly's wrist. Karly twisted away and moved to Butrus's other side. She whispered something in his ear, and Tarek watched with amusement as Butrus's eyes widened before he scowled.

"What was that about?" Adel asked as she walked away.

Butrus lifted his glass of vodka to his lips and took a sip without answering. There was an intense expression in Butrus's eyes that Tarek had never seen before.

"Good evening, gentlemen," Idella greeted. "I hope you are enjoying yourselves."

All three men rose to their feet. Idella raised an eyebrow at Butrus's unhappy expression.

"Whatever you would like... within reason, of course... is on the house tonight," she informed the two bodyguards. "The chef has prepared some delicious meals, and if you don't mind, I'll steal Tarek away for the night."

"We plan on having a great evening," Adel said.

"Oh, for sure," Butrus agreed.

Tarek laced his fingers with Idella's and followed her to the rooftop atrium. The moment the doors closed behind him, he swung her around, held her arms behind her back, and pressed her body against his. She gasped and their lips met in several passionate kisses.

"A week... you took a week to get back here," he growled, releasing her to cup her face.

"I... had to take care of a few things."

She tilted her head back, and he kissed the column of her neck. "If you ever do that again," he muttered.

"What will you do?" she asked.

The sparkle of delight in her eyes sent his blood boiling. His eyes lit on an extra-wide lounge covered in silk sheets. Near it, a table was set for two, decorated with lit candles. It took a moment for him to register the soft chords of music playing in the background and realize that she had arranged for this romantic setting.

"How likely are we to be interrupted?"

Her throaty laugh made him ache. "I've informed Midnight, Buddy, and the rest of my crew that I'm indisposed until further notice. The chefs are waiting for my call."

Tarek slid his hand up her back, grasped the zipper on her beautiful royal blue gown, and slowly pulled it down. Her uneven breaths matched his. The gown pooled around her slender ankles. She was bare underneath. She wasn't even wearing a pair of lacy panties.

"You were expecting me," he murmured with approval.

She lifted her chin. "And now *you* are overdressed."

"I need to be right now or I'll never last," he replied in a tortured voice.

Tarek scooped her up in his arms and carried her over to the chaise lounge. When he laid her down, he gazed at her body with hooded eyes and groaned. With a curse, he undressed.

"What about not being able to last?" she teased.

"Later… I'll worry about lasting later," he promised, bending over her with blazing eyes.

An hour later, they both relaxed at the table as Karly placed their meals in front of them. Idella had slipped on a beautiful, emerald silk kimono with large imprints of delicate orchids. Tarek was fully dressed in his black slacks and black dress shirt. Idella lifted her glass, laughing as she shared an antic from a guest earlier.

Tarek grinned, looked into her eyes, and said, "Marry me."

Idella's laugh trailed off, her eyes widening, and her breath hitching. He could not have held this back a moment longer if he tried. The decision began to blossom the first night they made love in London and solidified when they were in Simdan. He had wanted to ask her before she went on the mission to Coldhouse's compound, but didn't want to distract her. Now, Colin Coldhouse and Andrius Bronislav were still an issue, but they were a contained issue, held up at Bronislav's estate outside of Moscow.

Idella slowly lowered her glass to the table. She swallowed, and a mental wall came down between them, her luminous hazel eyes shielded by her eyelashes as she dropped her gaze to the glass in her hand.

"Tarek," she murmured.

He leaned forward and covered her hand. "Hear me out. I love you, and I know you love me. I know about your life… both of them. I will not try to stop you from being who you are. I want to be a part of it. I could no more ask you to stop being Dallas than you could ask me to quit being a sheikh. We are who we are destined to be," he said in a low, steady voice.

"Harlem…" she began, her voice soft and despairing.

Tarek shook his head. "Harlem said what worked for Harlem. This— you and I—we work for us. We make our own rules, our own decisions. We have our own baggage, and I am willing to help you carry yours. It's ok to give yourself to me, Idella. I am yours."

She pulled her hand from under his and walked over to the glass wall that had a view of the city. Her arms curled around her waist.

"I never thought… dreamed… of getting married. I always expected death would find me before love ever would."

He came to a stop close behind her, offering her his warmth without touching her. She sighed and leaned back against him. Sliding his hands along her hips, he molded himself against her back and covered her hands with his.

"Dare to dream, Idella. It could be reality," he murmured, lightly kissing the spot behind her ear.

Her chest expanded as she breathed in. She exhaled a long sigh. Tarek tightened his arms around her, threading his fingers through hers.

"How… do you imagine our marriage?" she asked.

He kissed her again—just a feathery caress while he breathed in her intoxicating scent.

"Our marriage will be full of adventure. Neither one of us is the type to live a quiet, normal life. We will fight for Jawahir … and I imagine other places in the world, but I hope you will no longer go on missions alone. We can use our power and skills differently. You'll be my partner in life, in my bed, and by my side as we face whatever obstacles life throws at us."

She was silent as she stared at the city. He could see their reflection in the glass, but it was not like looking into her eyes. After a minute, she guided his hands from her waist to her abdomen.

"And children?"

An unexpected pang of longing hit him. *Children!* He had never really thought about it. He knew Qadir would, but for himself... he had never believed he would fall in love, nevermind....

"How... do you feel about them?" he cautiously asked.

Her body shook with her silent laughter. "Answering a question with a question is the surest way to say that you don't want to answer," she teased.

"Well, I need to know a few things first," he replied, turning her in his arms so he could see her face. "Things like how soon do you want to start trying and how many—unless, you are trying to tell me we might have already started one? It isn't like I've been using protection."

Her eyes glittered with emotion. "We haven't. Started one, that is. I've been on the pill for a few years."

He tucked a strand of her hair behind her ear. "If you were pregnant, I would be over the moon, but only if you want to have a child. You come first. If being with you means no children, I choose you. If you will never give up your line of work, I choose you. I love you, *habibi*. You will always come first for me. I will always choose you."

He reached into his pocket and grasped the small velvet black box. Holding her hand, he lowered himself to one knee and looked up into her bemused eyes.

"Idella, will you do me the honor of accepting me as your husband?"

Her hand trembled in his and tears made her eyes glitter more brightly than the diamonds in the platinum band. She nodded.

"I would be honored to marry you, Tarek," she replied.

Tarek slid the intricate diamond and emerald ring onto her finger and surged to his feet in relief and joy. He wrapped his arms around her waist and swung her in a circle. The music of her laughter filled the atrium.

"I love you, Tarek," she breathed, sliding down his body.

"My *'amirat khurafia,*" he murmured before their lips met in soft steamy kisses that he never wanted to stop.

Epilogue

One month later:

Tarek's Bedroom, Jawahir Palace

Idella rolled over, her hand sweeping out to caress Tarek. Her hand touched cool sheets. She sat up and wildly searched the room until she noticed the muted sound of Tarek speaking to someone on the balcony.

"Reports are coming in.... I know, but.... Junayd, you aren't used to dealing with this.... I know, I know.... Just... make sure your guards are aware.... Alright. I'll see you when you return. Be safe, brother."

Idella swung her legs over the side of the bed and stood up. Grabbing the silk robe lying on the chair, she pulled it on to cover her nudity and moved to the balcony. She leaned against the doorframe, arching her back slightly and resting her hands behind her. The move parted the front of her robe until only a thin section strategically covered her breasts down to the top of her thighs. Tarek turned, an appreciative smile on his lips.

"Is there a problem?" she inquired.

"Nothing that Intelligence can't deal with," he answered, his eyes moving over her with desire.

"What happened?" she asked.

"Junayd is in New York. He is touring some of the medical facilities there."

"And...," she said.

"And... everything is under control," he promised, opening his arms to her.

Idella straightened and walked over to him. It was impossible to keep her eyes from roaming over his muscular frame. He had pulled on a pair of white sleep trousers that sat low on his hips, giving her a peek at the tantalizing dark hair that disappeared beneath the waistband.

The scar on his side has healed nicely, she thought, running her fingers along it.

Memories flooded her of running her hands through his tousled hair as he made love to her last night. She hummed with contentment and heat as his arms enfolded her. Her fingers slid up his muscular abs and she raked the dark hair covering his chest.

"If you keep looking at me like that, we'll be late for breakfast with my family."

"Breakfast is highly overrated, don't you think?" she murmured against his lips.

Her teasing answer earned her a passionate kiss that ended with her arms above her head and her body pressed against the wall. She wiggled against the evidence of his desire and tilted her head back as his mouth slid along the column of her throat. The tie of her robe loosened and the front opened. Her bare breasts pressed against the rough hair of his chest.

"Breakfast," she teased him in a breathy sing-song voice.

"We'll join them for lunch," he murmured.

"We were beginning to wonder if you two were still alive," Qadir called out as they entered the family dining room later that afternoon.

Idella blushed and slightly lifted her chin. Rosy cheeks could be glamorous, not a sign of embarrassment.

"Hello, Aimee. How was your morning?" Tarek asked.

Aimee gave him a brilliant smile, her eyes dancing with mirth. "Fabulous. We missed breakfast, too, by the way."

Tarek shot his older brother a raised eyebrow. Qadir shrugged and tried to look innocent. Chuckles from his parents brought color to both Princes' cheeks.

"Is it just me or is it getting hot in here?" Jameel complained, looking up from the tablet he had been utterly engrossed in with a puzzled frown.

"Oh, it's definitely getting warmer," Idella remarked.

Melik shook his head at his youngest son. "Jameel, can you pull yourself away from the screen long enough to be polite?" he asked with a disapproving scowl.

Jameel reluctantly flipped the screen over, but not before Idella noticed the bugs crawling across it, making a heart. She lifted an inquiring eyebrow. This time it was Jameel who blushed. He shifted uncomfortably in his seat before focusing on what his mother was saying.

"Idella, have you and Tarek decided when you'll marry?"

Idella smiled and looked at Tarek. "We were thinking of doing a small ceremony as soon as possible. I know it is sudden, but we don't want to wait."

"We could always have a double wedding," Aimee suggested. "Unless, you don't think that is a good idea."

"I think that is a marvelous idea! Honestly, I'd be happy if we were the only ones there, but Wallace, my manager, would hunt me down," Idella replied with a grimace.

For the rest of lunch, the women's discussion revolved around weddings while the men discussed the civil war raging in Simdan. Idella was far more interested in what was happening with Raja.

When she felt Ihab and Aimee looking at her, it took her brain a half-second to catch up with the conversation she was supposed to be focused on and realize that Ihab had asked her if she would mind her future mother-in-law taking over some of the planning for the weddings.

"I would love it. Honestly, Wallace handles all of my performance stuff. I just show up and sing. My expertise is not in organizing."

Ihab's eyes twinkled with delight—and knowledge. Ihab reached over and squeezed her hand. The expression in the older woman's eyes was soft and filled with understanding.

"Melik and I will always be here for you and do everything we can to support you. I love that you and Aimee have made my sons happy. This is a treasured gift to any parent."

The tension melted from Idella when she saw acceptance and genuine warmth in Ihab's eyes. Aimee's eyes glistened with tears and she brushed them away with an embarrassed laugh.

"Hormones! Wait until you and Tarek decide to have kids. Ihab says this is natural," Aimee choked.

Almost immediately, Qadir was at Aimee's side. He leaned over and murmured to Aimee who nodded and rose to her feet. She gave them an apologetic smile before excusing herself.

"Idella, are you ready?" Tarek asked.

Idella nodded and rose. "Thank you so much for all your help, Ihab. Please let me know when you'd like to meet to go over the details," she said.

"I will. The good thing about being the Queen of a country is that I have the best wedding planners at my fingertips," Ihab laughed.

"We'll see you later, mama," Tarek said, bending and kissing his mother on both cheeks.

Idella was quiet as they walked together, her thoughts all over the place but mostly centered on Raja.

"My family loves you almost as much as I do," Tarek assured, "and my youngest brothers have been warned to be on their best behavior."

"What *worst* behavior were you worried about?" Idella asked with amusement.

"Once Junayd and Jameel knew that Aimee was off-limits, I had to threaten them to keep their more *romantic* appreciation away from you," Tarek ruefully replied.

Laughter bubbled over as she remembered the twins making a beeline for her before suddenly veering off with sheepish grins. Now she understood the thunderous expression on Tarek's face.

"No one knows you as anything other than Idella—at the moment. It may become necessary in the future to share your identity with my family, but only as a security precaution. I can promise you that no one else will be aware. I will not tell them without your approval," he pledged.

"Thank you, though, something tells me that maybe your parents *do* know more than they let on. I've been meaning to tell you that my handler knows I've been compromised. The decision has been made to release me as I have become a liability."

He frowned. "When did you learn of this?"

Her lips curled into a wry smile. "Officially? Last night. Unofficially? The moment I chose to help a member of the Jawahir royal family instead of going after my target."

Tarek closed his eyes and leaned his forehead against hers. She caressed his cheek with one hand while her other lay over his pounding heart. A shudder ran through his body and he slowly opened his eyes.

"Are you alright?" he asked.

"Yes. I've never been more sure of anything in my life," she promised with a smile. Truer words had never been spoken. She had a full life now, and she was going to live it on her own terms with the man she loved at her side.

*Ready to read <u>**Midnight Shadows**</u>,*

Book 3 of the Girls from the Street series?

The next page has a sneak peek!

Midnight Shadows

GIRLS FROM THE STREET BOOK 3

Junayd waited until everyone was gone before he faced the hundred-year-old tree. Shoving his hands into his coat pockets, he slowly walked around the tree, carefully scanning the darkness for any sign of movement. The minutes stretched in silence and he began to wonder if perhaps he was mistaken. He stopped on the opposite side of the tree. A low branch curved toward the ground before reaching upward.

"You broke his arm," he said, waiting to see if the shadow would respond.

"He deserved it—and more," a soft voice replied.

Junayd twisted, trying to pinpoint the location of the speaker. His eyes locked on a tall hedge.

He took a step toward it and stopped. "You're right. In my country, in the desert, I would have killed him for abusing a woman like that," Junayd responded.

"Not a woman, a child. By the time I'm done with him, he'll wish he was in your desert."

The lilting sound of her voice caressed his senses. Shock filtered through him when he realized that the speaker was a woman. His body responded to the husky voice as if she were whispering directly to his soul.

"Who are you?" he demanded

"I'm vengeance, justice, someone's lost conscience."

She was all around him. No matter where he turned, he sensed she had moved, though he couldn't quite see her. She was like the *zala alqamar aleayim,* the floating moon shadow that swept across the dunes at night, making them appear alive.

"Pick whichever name you want," she replied.

"*I want….*" he said huskily.

The words were pulled from him before he had finished the thought, and saying them out loud brought him to a confused halt. He did not know what it was that he wanted, but he *wanted* something.

"What do you want, Dr. Junayd Saif-Ad-Din?"

He breathed in her mesmeric voice and slowly turned toward the trunk of the tree, captivated by the tantalizing scent of oranges and vanilla washing over his senses. His breath hissed when she stepped into a sliver of moonlight filtering through the barren branches of the old oak.

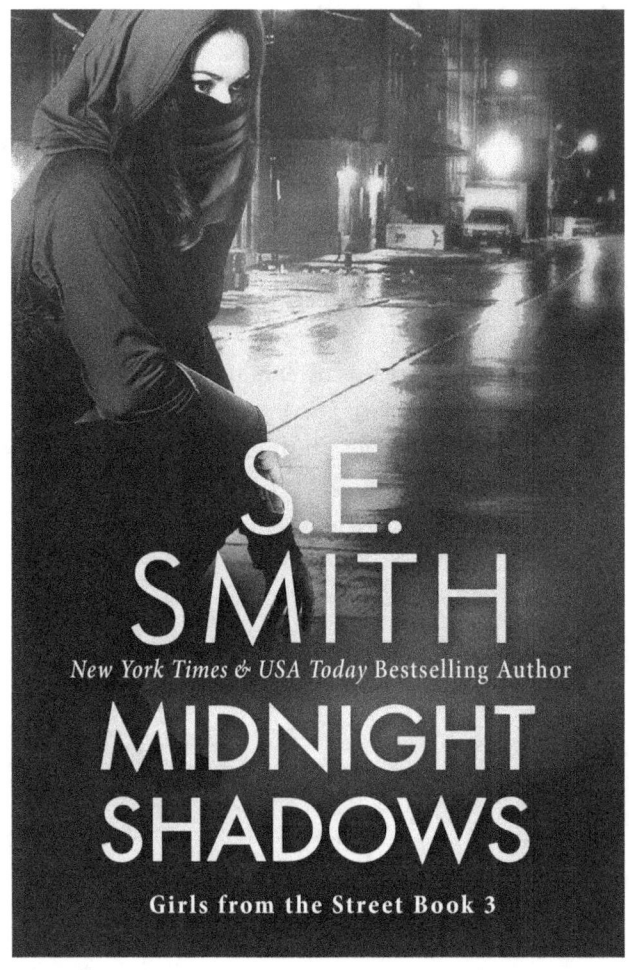

She was born on the streets; he was born to rule…

Sheikh Junayd Saif-Ad-Din wears the royal, sophisticated persona of wealth and power. He became a doctor to help his people, but his bloodline comes from the desert and a long line of warriors. His decorous veneer dissolves when he witnesses an attack while at a society function—and meets a mysterious woman who emerges from the darkness.

Despite living in a time when staying under the radar is a monumental task, Midnight Rain moves through society as an apparition. Her life was forged by the fires of the streets and she makes her living protecting others. She lives by just two rules: she only works at night and she tries to stay alive.

Junayd is determined to find the enigmatic woman who appeared from out of the night. Positive that she is his Chosen, the woman he is destined to love, Junayd will use every resource available to find her.

From the dark streets of New York City to the beautiful desert kingdom of Jawahir, danger hunts Midnight and Junayd. Can two modern-day warriors, one who lives in the shadows and one who thrives in the bright light of the desert, defeat a deranged man intent on killing them?

Girls from the Street Series

Novellas:
YOLANDA'S RAY OF SUNSHINE

Full-Length Books:
SOMETHING ABOUT AIMEE

COLOURS OF THE SOUL

MIDNIGHT SHADOWS

KATIE AND THE WARRIOR KING

THE GEEK AND THE SHEIKH

Additional Books

If you loved this story by me (S.E. Smith) please leave a review! You can discover additional books at: https://sesmithfl.com and https://sesmithya.com or find your favorite way to keep in touch here: https://sesmithfl.com/contact-me/ Be sure to sign up for my newsletter to hear about new releases!

Recommended Reading Order Lists:

https://sesmithfl.com/reading-list-by-events/

https://sesmithfl.com/reading-list-by-series/

The Series

Science Fiction / Romance

DRAGON LORDS OF VALDIER SERIES

It all started with a king who crashed on Earth, desperately hurt. He inadvertently discovered a species that would save his own.

CURIZAN WARRIOR SERIES

The Curizans have a secret, kept even from their closest allies, but even they are not immune to the draw of a little known species from an isolated planet called Earth.

MARASTIN DOW WARRIORS SERIES

The Marastin Dow are reviled and feared for their ruthlessness, but not all want to live a life of murder. Some wait for just the right time to escape....

SARAFIN WARRIORS SERIES

A hilariously ridiculous human family who happen to be quite formidable... and a secret hidden on Earth. The origin of the Sarafin species is more than it seems. Those cat-shifting aliens won't know what hit them!

DRAGONLINGS OF VALDIER NOVELLAS

The Valdier, Sarafin, and Curizan Lords had children who just cannot stop getting into trouble! There is nothing as cute or funny as magical, shapeshifting kids, and nothing as heartwarming as family.

Cosmos' Gateway Series

Cosmos created a portal between his lab and the warriors of Prime. Discover new worlds, new species, and outrageous adventures as secrets are unravelled and bridges are crossed.

The Alliance Series

When Earth received its first visitors from space, the planet was thrown into a panicked chaos. The Trivators came to bring Earth into the Alliance of Star Systems, but now they must take control to prevent the humans from destroying themselves. No one was prepared for how the humans will affect the Trivators, though, starting with a family of three sisters….

Lords of Kassis Series

It began with a random abduction and a stowaway, and yet, somehow, the Kassisans knew the humans were coming long before now. The fate of more than one world hangs in the balance, and time is not always linear….

Zion Warriors Series

Time travel, epic heroics, and love beyond measure. Sci-fi adventures with heart and soul, laughter, and awe-inspiring discovery…

Paranormal / Fantasy / Romance

Magic, New Mexico Series

Within New Mexico is a small town named Magic, an… <u>unusual</u> town, to say the least. With no beginning and no end, spanning genres, authors, and universes, hilarity and drama combine to keep you on the edge of your seat!

Spirit Pass Series

There is a physical connection between two times. Follow the stories of those who travel back and forth. These westerns are as wild as they come!

Second Chance Series

Stand-alone worlds featuring a woman who remembers her own death. Fiery and mysterious, these books will steal your heart.

More Than Human Series

Long ago there was a war on Earth between shifters and humans. Humans lost, and today they know they will become extinct if something is not done....

The Fairy Tale Series

A twist on your favorite fairy tales!

A Seven Kingdoms Tale

Long ago, a strange entity came to the Seven Kingdoms to conquer and feed on their life force. It found a host, and she battled it within her body for centuries while destruction and devastation surrounded her. Our story begins when the end is near, and a portal is opened....

Epic Science Fiction / Action Adventure

Project Gliese 581G Series

An international team leave Earth to investigate a mysterious object in our solar system that was clearly made by <u>someone</u>, someone who isn't from Earth. Discover new worlds and conflicts in a sci-fi adventure sure to become your favorite!

New Adult / Young Adult

Breaking Free Series

A journey that will challenge everything she has ever believed about herself as danger reveals itself in sudden, heart-stopping moments.

The Dust Series

Fragments of a comet hit Earth, and Dust wakes to discover the world as he knew it is gone. It isn't the only thing that has changed, though, so has Dust...

About the Author

S.E. Smith is an *internationally acclaimed, New York Times* **and** **USA TODAY** *Bestselling* author of science fiction, romance, fantasy, paranormal, and contemporary works for adults, young adults, and children. She enjoys writing a wide variety of genres that pull her readers into worlds that take them away.

www.ingramcontent.com/pod-product-compliance
Lightning Source LLC
Chambersburg PA
CBHW050657290626
47170CB00015B/1599